Surprised by Old Age

May Paddock

SURPRISED BY OLD AGE

Cover Photo: Jefferson Eliot
Cover Design: Jefferson Eliot

Edited by: Rosemary Ahern

Website developed by Tom Stier

Visit the author website:
http://www.maypaddock.com

ISBN: ISBN: **978-1-939980-25-0** (ebook)
ISBN: ISBN: **978-1-939980-24-3** (paperback)

Published by: WriteSpa Press

Version: 2025.05.05

In Memory of

Ethel Cook Eliot

Chapter One

Paul clutched the rosary beads he found in his hand. He tried to focus on one bead at a time to unearth a prayer from below his fear. The air was thick with disinfectant. He needed to get out of bed to find and open a window, but to his growing horror, his legs wouldn't move.

To subdue his rising panic he imagined himself home in the streets of Mérida where the tapping of his cane added to the honking of trucks, the shouts of shopkeepers calling out their wares, and the greetings from unseen friends: "Let me put some fruit in your sack, please Father." "Father, are you coming to my house?" "Feel my hand that you blessed, Father. It is healed."

Paul was brought back into the present by a knock on a door. Then a woman approached, mumbling a prayer in English. She smelled of cigarette smoke, and her shoes made a funny squeak. Paul heard the rustle of her clothes and guessed that she was a nun in full habit. She said nothing as she took his hand and felt for his pulse not gently or roughly, but practically, as though his hand had no connection to his arm or to him. Paul tried to ask her something, but before he could get the words out, his hand was placed on his chest, as though he were a corpse, and he heard her squeaking and rustling away. Then the door closed with a thud.

For a long time there was silence. The air smelled more and more toxic. Paul felt that he was being smothered by a pillow of poison.

Then came another knock. The door was opened and Paul heard the squeak of the nun's shoes and the rustle of her habit, but behind all that he heard heavier footsteps. "Father Brown" the nun said, too loudly after all that silence, "Do you feel well enough for a visitor?"

Paul opened his mouth to get the answer out before the visitor retreated, but then he heard Joe say, "I'll just sit with him for a while. Thank you, Sister."

"Don't let him get too tired."

"I won't."

Paul let his head fall back on the pillow. Joe, whom he'd last been with years ago at the Cathedral in Mérida, was here! Paul felt as though he'd fallen overboard in a stormy sea and Joe had thrown him a lifeline. Fresh air and the smell of recently cut grass clung to Joe's clothes. His breath smelled of hamburger with red onion. He drew up a chair next to the bed, and put his instrument on the floor beside the chair. "It's Joe Wilson Father. Do you feel strong enough to talk? I brought my oboe if you'd rather I play for you."

"Where are we?" It took a while for Paul to get the words out, but Joe was patient.

"Do you know that you're in the All Souls Retreat House in Upstate New York?"

Paul shook his head slightly.

"You had a stroke in Mérida and they sent you here to recover.

"Can you open a window?"

"Let's see." Joe got up and moved away. Paul heard the sound of a window being raised and then he felt the fresh air rush in. He breathed deeply. *I'm going to live,* he told himself.

When Joe sat down again next to the bed, Paul said, "Please play."

"Do you think I should ask permission from the Sister?"

"No."

Joe pushed back his chair a little. Paul heard him take the pieces of his oboe out of the case and put them together. Joe sighed briefly, and then took a large breath and began to play.

The music carried Paul off the bed and out of the window to early summer days in Mexico when the rain, the glorious precious rain, washed the streets, drenched the fields, and filled the water tanks. Then the music took him home to summers in Harlem. Someone had opened a fire hydrant. Children stood in its spray in their underwear and danced as the water cooled them from head to toe. The children chased around Paul. He stretched and danced in place knowing that the children, no matter how wild their play, were always watching out for him.

After a third sharp knock on the door, Joe stopped

playing. The nun, sounding much too loud said, "That's very nice, but I think it may make my patient too excited. Also the clergy who are studying or at prayer may find it disturbing."

"I apologize, Sister, if I've disturbed...

But Joe was interrupted, "That was glorious! That should make you feel better, eh Father?"

"Yes!" Paul said as loudly as possible though it sounded like a whisper. Bits of memory were coming back. Paul had heard this voice before.

"Good for you. It certainly gave me a lift." Then the voice addressed Joe, "Are you an old friend of Father Paul's?"

"Father Paul saved my life about a decade ago in Mexico."

"Well, and now you're bringing him back to life here. Don't let me interrupt you. I'm going to leave this door, and the door to my office, open; I'm grateful for your beautiful playing. Aren't you Sister?"

"Yes, Father." Paul heard her habit rustle sharply as her shoes squeaked out of the room followed by the priest's more leisurely footsteps.

Joe began to play again, but Paul fell asleep. He didn't hear Joe leave, but he vaguely remembered a friendly hand on his shoulder.

Chapter Two

As Paul's body inched its way towards movement, he felt less despair but growing irritation. He hated that he needed the nun's help in order to turn over in bed, and that she was obliged to feed him spoonful by spoonful as though he were an infant. He hated that he couldn't reach for his rosary even though it was under his pillow, but had to wait for someone to put it in his hand.

And worst of all he hated his hatred. For decades he had tried to help people accept their lives and rediscover their strengths by knowing that God was always with them. The fact that Paul now kept forgetting that God was near as he struggled against his paralysis made Paul feel that all this time he had been a humbug, a hypocrite, a fake. Paul hated himself most of all.

In time his anger, and overwhelming doubt about himself, slowly waned as Sister Josephine taught him how to stretch his fingers, his toes, his hands and feet until they became, at long last, obedient to his wishes. Then he began to be able to move his arms and legs, very cautiously at first. The great day was when Paul managed to get from his bed onto the wheelchair.

Paul heard Sister Josephine chuckle at that

accomplishment with what he realized, after a startled moment, was pride and happiness. "We did it, didn't we," she said.

"We did indeed," Paul answered, truly grateful for the first time for all her ministrations.

A few weeks later when he was able to push himself up from the wheelchair and take a few steps holding on to a walker, he heard her gasp with joy. "I can't thank you enough, Sister," he said quickly.

"It has all been my pleasure, Father" was her gentle response.

As Paul learned how to maneuver the walker, he began to wander the halls of All Souls. First he found his way to the chapel. He spent long hours there learning how to forgive himself for his anger, and sometimes having helpful conversations with other priests struggling with ill health.

Then he began to explore further afield, remembering the turns right and left so he could find his way back to the chapel, and from there back to the infirmary.

These explorations reminded him of the day of his eighth birthday. He had been blinded about six months before. On this day his father taught him how to use his new white cane, and then asked him to do an errand for the family, to buy a bottle of milk from the grocery store around the corner.

Chapter Three

The next time Joe visited he told Paul that he was composing a duet for oboe and piano, "but so far I've only developed the oboe part."

"I know where there's a piano," Paul said. "I've been wheeling myself all over this place, exploring it as though it were a foreign country. I found a room with an upright piano and it's more or less in tune. Let's go there. I can play some chords and you can see if they give you ideas for the piano part?"

"Yes indeed!" Joe exclaimed. "I had no idea you played."

As they made their way to another wing of the building, Paul told Joe about being taught how to play the piano by Gerald Cohen, a volunteer at The Lighthouse for the Blind.

"I've been here every day since I found this room," Paul said as he maneuvered himself off the wheelchair and onto the piano stool.

Joe played through what he'd written for the oboe. He played it again while Paul explored possible chords. Despite the complete darkness that surrounded Paul, as he played he felt as though he and Joe were hiking in the mountains with long magnificent views, shadowy tree-covered valleys, and huge boulders to climb over. He was free of his frail body and his blindness.

A few hours later, as they walked and rolled back to the infirmary, they were stopped at the door by Sister Josephine. "Well Father I'm going to have to kick you out. I have a new patient who is contagious. We've moved your stuff to a room down the hall. You're the third door on the left."

"Thank you, Sister," was all Paul said, but inside he was shouting *Alleluia Alleluia* as he slid his hand along the wall and counted off the doors.

Chapter Four

That evening Father Gregory came to visit Paul in his private room. He looked around and saw that Paul had unpacked the suitcase that had been sent with him from the Cathedral in Mérida. "I hope you're not going to feel lonely in this room? I know Sister Josephine made things as comfortable as possible in the infirmary."

"She certainly did! But I'm very grateful to be on my own."

"Yes I can imagine. Listen, I have two messages for you. Father Jorge called from the Cathedral in Mérida and was relieved and pleased to hear how well you are doing. And I talked with your oboist friend, Joe, about transportation. We no longer have a physician at All Souls, but there's an excellent doctor in Albany whom we work with. Joe has arranged for a young man named Michael to drive you there for your first appointment tomorrow afternoon."

The next afternoon there was a gentle knock on Paul's door. "Come in!" Paul called out, grateful that his voice was back.

"Father, a young man has arrived and parked by the side door. He asked me to tell you that he's at your service."

"Thank you. Would you please tell him I'll be right there?"

Paul picked up his jacket, checked that his wallet was in

the pocket, grabbed his walker, and made his way to the side door where there was a ramp. When he managed to get the heavy door open, the young man stepped back out of the way and asked, "Father Brown?"

"You must be Michael."

"Yes sir. I parked the car close by. Do you need help?"

"No thank you, Michael. When we get closer to your car, you can show me where the door is."

"Okay, but it's not really my car. My grandmother's friend, Seamus, loaned it to me.

"Please tell Seamus that I'm grateful." Paul stood still with his face turned toward the sun breathing in the wonderful smell of recently cut grass, and listening to the birds calling back and forth. He whispered a prayer of gratitude.

Michael waited for Paul in a silence that felt friendly. When they got down the ramp to the car, Michael carefully helped Paul fold himself into the front seat. He folded the walker into the back seat and then got in himself. When Paul told him the address, Michael said, "I already went there. It'll be a piece of cake."

"You sound well prepared."

"I figured since you can't read the map, I should make sure I knew how to get there."

"Good figuring. Have you been taking many people places?"

"Just Seamus and my grandmother. As soon as I got a permit, I drove Seamus all over the county, even on the highway. Seamus helps migrant farm workers. Once I learn enough Spanish, I can drive them places on my own."

"I wish I'd studied Spanish before I was sent to Mexico."

"What did you do in Mexico?"

"I was a priest there for many years."

"Could you see then?"

"No, I lost my eyesight when I was seven. I was hit by a car."

"But you could be a priest?"

"It wasn't the blindness that got in my way when I first went to Mexico, it was not knowing Spanish well enough. It took a lot of careful listening to find my way into the language and then to find my way along the streets of the city."

"I lived for years in Bombay. Now it's called Mumbai. You should see what those narrow winding streets are like." After a few minutes of silence Michael asked, "Am I saying something awful when I say things like 'you should see'?"

"Not at all. People say it all the time and then I feel them wincing. Since most people learn things by seeing, it's a much used expression."

"How do you learn things?"

"Listening to what people say and how they say it, and listening to whatever sounds are around me at the time. Sometimes I'm allowed to feel things with my hands, and that can be a big help. Also of course there are smells. Plus I know how to read braille, so I can learn about things far off in time or space."

"My grandmother showed me a book printed in braille. I couldn't distinguish the bumps well enough to know that one letter was different from another. That must be slow reading."

"It was when I started, but after a while you begin to speed up."

"Can you read braille in Spanish?"

"Now I can, but it took a while to learn it. What language did you speak when you were living in Mumbai?"

"Mostly English. I learned a few words in Hindi from the people in stores, and from playing games during recess, but basically it was English." They drove in silence for a while. Michael was finding his way through city traffic and Paul didn't want to distract him. Finally Michael pulled the car over to the curb with a cheerful "Here we are!"

He got the walker out of the back seat. As Paul slowly climbed out of the car, Michael asked, "Do you want me to go in with you?"

"As far as the waiting room."

Paul knew immediately that the doctor he'd been assigned was very young. She called him Father in every other sentence and was awkward and embarrassed as she asked questions about his personal habits and abilities. Finally she suggested that Paul see a neurologist and a cardiologist, have a bone scan, a fasting blood test, and an EKG.

As Michael carefully drove them back to All Souls

through the city traffic, Paul said, "It looks as though there are going to be lots of other doctor appointments. Do you think you could ask Seamus if you'd be able to borrow his car again? I'd be more than happy to pay him for the gas and to pay you for your time."

"I'll ask Seamus. I don't think there will be a difficulty. Someone recently gave him an old van so he can take five or six people at a time to clinics." After they drove on in silence for a while, Michael added, "I'd rather you didn't pay me for my time. Maybe instead, you could talk to me really slowly in Spanish. That would be a big help. I can be Seamus's assistant once I'm fluent in Spanish."

"I'm happy to talk to you slowly in Spanish and pay you as well," Paul told him.

After more silence, Michael said, "If you're not paying me, I could suggest we go other places. Like there's a big waterfall where we can climb down stone steps and get close to it. And Seamus told me that Franklin Roosevelt lived not far from here and we can visit his house. And there's a lake where we can rent rowboats…"

"Eleanor Roosevelt is one of my heroes; I would like immensely to visit their house."

"Okay!" Michael said. And Paul heard the smile in his voice.

Chapter Five

Despite the many tests and visits to specialists, Paul's doctor seemed annoyed that Paul wasn't responding to the medicines the way she thought he should. By the time Paul got back to the waiting room after a long visit with her, he hurried Michael out of the office, and didn't breathe deeply until they were on the sidewalk.

"Are you in a hurry to get back? Does Seamus need the car?"

"No, Seamus is using the van. Do you want to go somewhere?"

"You mentioned renting a rowboat somewhere near here?"

"Yes there's a lake. There aren't any motorboats on it, just rowboats and canoes."

"I would very much like to go out onto a lake."

"Okay, let's do it!"

As Michael drove, Paul remembered his one experience of being in a rowboat. It was on a lake in Central Park. He was six. He was with a friend from school and the friend's mother. She told the boys to sit together on the bench in the stern and she sat in the middle of the boat and rowed. She said that their job was to look and tell her what was ahead of them because she had her back to the direction in which they were going.

That was perhaps the last time that anyone ever asked Paul to be helpful by looking.

Now he was again wrapped in a life jacket, "We wouldn't want you to grab for it and not find it, Father," said the man who was renting them the boat.

"Do you want to row?" Michael asked as they were getting into the boat.

"Yes" Paul said, feeling that the oars had thick rings around them so they wouldn't slip out of their holders. "If you'll keep me from crashing into anyone."

"I'll do that."

The oars felt warm and heavy and friendly in Paul's hands. He began to dip them deeper and deeper into the water. He loved the sound of the water falling away from them as he pushed down on the ends he was holding in order to lift the blades out of the water. He didn't know how far they were moving with each dip but Michael assured him, "There are no other rowers out right now!"

As he created a rhythm and felt the rowboat respond to his every move, Paul felt as though his body was waking up after a long sleep.

He was heading, Michael told him, toward the middle of the lake. As Paul rowed he felt as though he was pushing his horizons out farther and farther away, making more room to expand into.

"We're now at the very center of the lake," Michael told him.

 Without saying anything, Paul lifted his oars and rested their handles inside the boat. Michael didn't speak either. Together they listened to the silence.

The birds whose singing couldn't be heard while Paul rowed, now seemed to be welcoming him and Michael into their world.

Paul and Michael sat together in silence in their slightly rocking boat. No need to say a word. Being together made their joy all the greater.

After a while they heard other rowers and boats coming toward them. Paul suggested that they change places so that Michael could row them back. "I've loved not needing to worry about bumping into anyone."

"This'll be a little different," Michael said.

On the return trip Paul felt as though he was surrounded by an orchestra of oars and boats each with their own dipping and splashing rhythms. And there were the friendly conversations and bantering calls between the rowers. Somewhere far away a bell began to toll the hour. All of these, enhanced by the silence that he and Michael had experienced earlier, made Paul feel more open to whatever his doctor decided to share with him whenever she was ready to do so.

Chapter Six

Seamus loved hearing Michael's happy descriptions of his gallivants with Father Paul. He told Michael that he would like to meet Father Paul, and Michael gave him the phone number of All Souls. Seamus called to ask if Father Paul accepted visitors.

"Tell me your name please, and I'll find out."

In very few minutes the response was "Yes indeed, Father Paul will be happy to see you. Perhaps tomorrow at 4:00?"

Michael had drawn a large map for Seamus, clearly delighted that his two friends were going to know each other. Seamus followed the wide graveled driveway to the large red brick building that looked like a public school built in the 1950s, except that there was a fountain at the center of the turnaround of the driveway. In front of the building was a black priest in a wheelchair, talking with a nun in full habit.

Seamus parked his car and walked toward them to ask the whereabouts of Father Brown, but was greeted before he'd said a word by the priest, "Seamus, friend of Michael, I presume."

"Yes, indeed. But…"

"The gravel gave you away. You have the tread of a man one can depend on, but who has a slight limp. Also I was waiting for you. I want to introduce you to Sister Josephine, my great helper."

Seamus was about to put out his hand to the nun but noticed how her hands were well hidden and remembered that that was not the custom. "Pleased to meet you, Sister," he said instead.

"I thought it would be nice to sit outside, if that suited you," Father Paul continued. "I think you'll see a couple of chairs under the oak tree. I'm not so good on rough ground so Sister is ready to wheel me over there if that is difficult for you."

"Thank you Sister, but I'll be able to do that."

When they had settled under the trees, with Seamus's chair facing Father Paul's wheelchair, there were a few moments of comfortable silence before Seamus said, "I wanted to thank you for exploring this area with Michael. He comes home filled with joy after your adventures."

"It is you, Seamus, that makes our adventures possible by lending us your car. Michael is a wonderful companion, especially for a man without sight. He describes what we are looking at with an exactness and an enthusiasm that sometimes makes me feel that I am seeing it with him. I think one day he may become a well-known author.

"He tells me that he has been studying with you and his grandmother rather than going to high school, and that the three of you are getting him ready for college."

"He is doing most of that on his own. He's really been teaching himself these last four years. I didn't go to college myself, so he and I enjoy researching subjects that are new to both of us, like physics and ancient history, and then teaching each other what we have learned."

"Michael tells me that your late wife was a high school teacher."

"Yes, Rose started teaching at her alma mater as soon as she graduated from college. She was much loved."

"I'm sure she was. How long have you been widowed?"

"Eight years."

"That's a long time to be on one's own."

"I'm not really on my own. My daughter, Caitlin, and her friend, actually her partner, live nearby. And Michael's grandmother, Maggie, has become a special friend. Almost too special."

"Too special?"

"When Rose was dying, I told her I would never love anyone else, but now I find myself more and more attracted to Maggie despite what I promised."

Seamus was silent for a minute, as though his betrayal of Rose had just caught up with him, making him feel a little desperate. Then after a sigh, he said, "I'd already betrayed her in another way. Rose's brother, James, came with me into the police academy, against Rose's wishes. He was killed trying to protect people from a sniper five years later."

"Do you have an image of where Rose is now?"

Seamus felt confused by the question. Was there a right answer? If so, he didn't know what it was, so he mumbled, "Not really."

"Have you ever tried talking with her?" After waiting through a long silence, Father Paul continued, "Give yourself a place and a time when you won't be interrupted; tell her what you want her to know, and then listen."

"Listen?" Seamus asked.

"Yes, just listen, and see what happens."

A loud bell began to toil. "I'm sorry," Father Paul said, "I need to go to the service."

Sister Josephine came almost running, despite her age and weight, across the grass. "I'm sorry Father but I don't want them to have to wait for you. Are you ready?" With a quick nod at Seamus, she turned Father Paul's wheelchair around on its back two wheels and pushed him manfully toward the red brick building that looked like a children's school, but was in fact an old-age home for priests."

Father Paul called over his shoulder as he was bumped along, "If you'd like to meet again please call the office."

Chapter Seven

"Goodbye, goodbye."

"I love you Grandma. Don't lose my painting."

"Do you have my origami?"

"Thank you dear Joan for all you've done."

"Come back soon, Grandma. We'll come visit you, Grandma."

These were the words, except they were in Spanish, that surrounded Joan in the hot Managua airport, as she turned her back on her stepson, his wife, and their two boys, and headed toward the plane. Joan turned one last time to wave before she grabbed the almost burningly hot metal banister and started climbing toward the door of the plane.

Her seat was on the other side of the plane so she couldn't see her family when she sat down. She wouldn't have been able to see them anyway through her tears.

Joan hurried through the Houston Airport to catch her plane to Albany, New York. She felt almost affronted by the profusion of bright clothes, shiny leather luggage on wheels, and fluorescent advertisements for perfumes and trips to the Caribbean. She'd only been living in Nicaragua for a few years, but now her home country seemed gaudy beyond belief.

Seamus met her at the baggage claim. He was wonderfully familiar. He was her daughter-in-law's uncle and had visited them often in Nicaragua. He looked very much the way he had on his last visit, wearing khaki slacks, a short sleeved cotton shirt and a Notre Dame baseball cap. His hair and beard were turning grey, but he held himself very erect, despite his prosthetic foot. He had been a policeman most of his life.

"It's good to see you, Joan dear, Is everyone well in Malpaisillo?

"Yes, all is well and they all send their love. I've gifts for you from the boys: a portrait of a rooster from Ben and an origami creature from Toby."

"Wonderful. I'm so glad you were there for them. Maura wrote that she didn't know how she and Juan would have managed without you. I think she's a fool not to have you care for the new baby as well. I know of nothing more generous than your moving out of your house to make room for the nursery.

"Not that we," he quickly added, "aren't thrilled by your coming north. It just seems..."

"Yes, I know." Joan interrupted. "But now I'm looking forward to experiencing winter."

Seamus grunted. Joan wasn't fooling anybody. He put her suitcase into the back of his car and they drove to the village of Carleton.

On Main Street across from the movie theater was the

Village Café and next to it the Carleton Bookstore. Between the doors to the café and the bookstore was a narrow red door which Joan unlocked. They climbed the steep stairs to the second floor. Seamus moving slowly, gripping the banister with each step because of his prosthetic foot.

Joan unlocked the door to the apartment and they went in. The apartment was completely bare, beautiful with its high ceilings and tall windows looking out over Main Street.

But there was no furniture and she was exhausted. "When Sage wrote me that the apartment was vacant again, I never thought to ask ..."

"Come spend the night at my place," Seamus said quietly. "I'll be fine on the sofa. In the morning we'll round you up some furniture."

After a night of deep sleep in Seamus's narrow bed, with him on the sofa across the room, they breakfasted at a local diner.

After breakfast, Seamus handed Joan the keys to his car, "I'll use the van today," and told her about the local Catholic Church. "They store furniture for people in need."

An elderly lady with the help of her cane led Joan down steep stairs to a windowless room filled with sofas, beds, tables and chairs. "It looks as though these are the insides of apartments of people who fled for their lives," Joan opined.

"Yes, you're right. I know that some of the families were

fleeing deportation."

"How does the furniture come to be here?"

"The landlords take what they want and then give us a call. Shall I leave you to look around? Here are red stickers to put on anything you want. Our maintenance man, John, can deliver them to you this afternoon.

"Thank you," Joan said, "This is a wonderful service that you provide."

"You're very welcome, and perhaps you'll enjoy experiencing Mass with us on Sunday, I mean if you are part of our tradition," she added quickly.

"Yes, I am" Joan said vaguely, not having taken part in a church service for many years. "I look forward to it," she added.

"That's nice," the lady said politely. Just stop in at the office before you leave and we'll write down your address. You said it was in Carleton."

"Yes I'm upstairs above the Carleton Bookstore."

"That sounds like we'll need some strong volunteers to carry the things up."

By evening Joan was ensconced in her new/old apartment. She'd bought some pots and pans, and unpacked the clothes she'd brought with her from Malpaisillo. She stored them in a large wicker basket that a wine merchant was planning to throw out. Beside the basket were the three books she'd brought. Beside the books was a narrow bed made up with the sheets she'd brought with her, and her hand woven shawl as a blanket.

In the living room that looked out on Main Street she had a table and two chairs near the kitchen area. Facing one of the large windows was a bright blue wooden rocking chair that her landlady, Sage, had brought up from the bookstore below, "We've had three children get hurt as they managed to tip this chair over. It'll be much safer, and happier, here."

Chapter Eight

Years before, when Joan had decided to leave upstate New York and spend the rest of her life in Nicaragua, she'd given away everything she couldn't take with her. But she had not known what to do with an almost life-sized self portrait by her daughter, Angelica, a well-known painter, who had committed suicide a few months after painting it. The large canvas appeared to be entirely black when you first looked at it. Most people would then look away, but if one continued to look, one saw that the blackness was created by five overlapping black irregular triangles. At the bottom right hand corner of the canvas was a short blood-red line where Angelica's signature should have been. The Newbury Street Gallery in Boston had given Angelica a show weeks before her death. They had not sold this self portrait and they assumed that Joan would want to keep it.

Joan was horrified when they delivered it to her apartment. This was a painting she never wanted to see again. This painting yelled at her even when she wasn't looking at it. "Look how you failed me!"

Joan's son-in-law, Joe, had taken it off her hands. He taught at the private high school, The Academy, which was having an exhibit of works by local artists, and they were delighted to include it.

But about a week after Joan's return to Carleton, when she arrived home after a walk, and climbed the steep stairs to her apartment, she found the horrendous self portrait leaning against her door with a note from Joe. "Welcome home Joan! So glad you're back! The Academy thanks you very much for your loan. Looking forward to seeing you soon, Joe"

Joan had felt peacefully happy walking between the fields on a road west of Carleton, but now her stomach groaned within her. She turned the portrait to face the wall and went inside the apartment, locking her door as though the portrait might manage to follow her in.

It wasn't until the next morning, after two cups of coffee, that she decided she did not want to leave it in the hall. She could almost hear Angelica banging on the door to be let in. Joan retrieved the painting keeping the blank back towards her and set it up facing the wall between the two tall windows looking out on Main Street.

There was an urgent knocking on her door. "Come in" she shouted feeling confused.

Sage opened the door a crack and peeked in. "Am I disturbing you?"

"Not at all," Joan said, quickly wiping her eyes. "Would you like some coffee?"

"No thanks, I'm actually teaching a class, but my model for this afternoon's class just called to back out. Would it be at all possible for you to model for the class this afternoon? I'll take it off the rent."

"You mean naked?"

"No, no, you can wear what you're wearing now. I would appreciate it immensely, just this afternoon for about an hour and a half. Do you think you could?

"Okay."

"Wonderful. It's at two o'clock."

"I'll be there."

"You're an angel." And Sage closed the door. Joan heard her hurrying down the steep stairs.

Earlier that week, Sage had shown Joan around her studio. Joan especially liked Sage's brightly colored landscapes of places that were familiar. Sage made them look more interesting than Joan remembered them. Joan felt that the paintings were teaching her to look more intensely at wherever she saw.

This afternoon all of Sage's paintings faced the walls, and there were easels everywhere. Some were on tall tripods so that the students stood at them; others were lower so the students could sit as they worked. In the center of the large, airy, sunny room was a small area raised about six inches from the floor with a comfortable looking leather upholstered chair. That turned out to be Joan's spot. She was wearing red slacks and a white cotton turtleneck sweater. She did not want the students to paint her wrinkled old neck.

As soon as she entered the studio, the twelve or so

students stopped talking. Sage introduced her. "My friend, Joan Estrada, is volunteering for just this afternoon. I suggest we do three 15 minute poses with five minute breaks in between. Joan, if you would make yourself comfortable on the chair. Feel free to use the chair in any way that you want, lying on it, sitting on one arm, whatever, just as different as possible from the pose before."

"Okay." Joan stepped up onto the raised area and sat on the chair with her back against one arm and both her legs over the other arm.

"Perfect," Sage called out. "Let's get started."

Fifteen minutes turned out to be a very long time. In the beginning Joan tried very hard not to move at all, even making her breathing more shallow, but after a while she remembered that she wasn't playing dead, and a little movement, a little shifting to make herself comfortable, wasn't the end of the world. When the bell rang she got up gratefully and stretched, "May I look at what you've been doing?" she asked.

"Sure," "If you like," and "If you won't be angry," were some of the answers. So Joan stepped down off the dais, and walked behind some of the students and their easels. In some of the paintings Joan thought she looked a hundred years old. There was a painting of the backs of other students painting. And a painting of one of Joan's hands. There was a painting of just the colors of her clothes surrounded by the color of the chair she sat on. Joan realized that as a model she was like a diving board from which people could swim in whatever direction they wanted.

Chapter Nine

The next morning, after a lot of coffee, Joan felt courage rising up in her and she turned Angelica's painting away from the wall. She moved the blue rocking chair to face the portrait and sat down and stared at the five black intersecting triangles. After a while she wondered if the painting, rather than being a cry of despair, was actually Angelica's shout out of admiration to Ad Reinhard. As she stared, Joan slowly came to the decision to make her own portrait of Angelica.

Angelica had been beautiful when she was young, almost always on the edge of laughter. But after her father died when she was fifteen, Angelica began to hear voices, and from then on her expression was often on the edge of desperation.

Joan considered painting her in the denim overalls and red tee shirt that Angelica wore as a child most days during summer vacation. Her hair was cut as short as a boy's and she followed her father around whenever he was home. Angelica and her father loved baseball. Charles took the family to Fenway Park a few times each summer, but he and Angelica reveled in discussing the games and statistics throughout the season.

After making her decision, Joan drove the second hand Ford, that Seamus had helped her buy, into Hudson. She bought an easel, a stool, a little table, stretched canvases, brushes and paints.

At home she placed a stretched canvas on her new easel in the middle of the room. Facing it was her stool and the table holding her new paints and brushes.

"What about painting the real me?" This question in Angelica's voice echoed in Joan's head as she stared at the canvas. She decided to accept the dare and paint her portrait of Angelica as an adult.

Finally she began to sketch with a soft pencil.

Chapter Ten

The second time Joan modeled for Sage's class, she found that it was easier to stay still for the fifteen minute poses when she didn't try so hard. After having seen their work the week before, she no longer wondered what the students were thinking of her.

Her mind wandered to her developing portrait of Angelic. Not having a model to work from, she was creating an image in her imagination and trying to bring it forward onto the canvas. But Joan found that as she worked on Angelica's portrait, her image of Angelica kept changing. At first Joan had tried to hold it still in her memory, as though she could take a photograph of it there. But the image was fluid, as though Joan was looking at Angelica through the rain. Perhaps, Joan thought, she was looking at her image of Angelica through the tears she had shed again and again as Angelica became more desperate and more difficult to help.

It was a relief when Sage called, "Time! Thank you very much Joan. Have a good week everybody." Joan stood up and stretched and looked around.

As she stepped down from the dais, one of the older students approached her. "Thank you so much, Mrs. Estrada. I'm new to all of this, but I find you a wonderful model. My name is Alejandro Garcia. Would you have the kindness to join me for a cup of coffee in the café downstairs?"

Joan stared at him for a moment as she made up her mind — grey hair, black eyes lengthened with many laugh wrinkles, her height, latte colored skin, most likely from Latin America. "I'd be enchanted to do that" she answered in Spanish.

"Ah, how wonderful! We can speak in my mother tongue," he said in Spanish.

They settled themselves in a booth in the coffee shop. They ordered espressos, and with Alejandro's encouragement they added slices of apple pie to the order.

Speaking in Spanish, Alejandro told Joan that he was a Town Justice for the court in Hudson. When she asked if her friend, Seamus, had ever brought migrant farm workers in front of him, he said, "Yes indeed, for things like driving without a license. Of course these people cannot obtain a driver's license without a green card, so it's a real Catch 22."

Joan told Alejandro that her husband had been killed in the War Against the Contras, and that her stepson had fallen in love with Seamus's niece. "They're now married and living in my house in Nicaragua."

"My wife died last year, after a long battle with cancer. "I'm thinking of selling my house in Hudson. My term as a Justice will end in a few months and I do not plan to run again."

"What will you do instead?"

"Well I certainly plan to come back to more painting classes. Do you model for all of them?"

"No, I'm a substitute when there's no one else."

"And what do you do, may I ask, when you're not modeling?"

"I don't know yet. I'm finding my way. I have recently returned from Nicaragua where I was taking care of my stepson's children. I'm no longer needed there, so I'm exploring my options."

"Ah, that sounds as though we have both come to forks in the road."

"Yes, it certainly does."

As they shook hands goodbye in front of the café, Alejandro said, "I hope we can meet again and share our experiences of exploring our new paths."

Joan gave his hand a quick squeeze as she said, "I do too."

Chapter Eleven

The portrait of Angelica was beginning to feel to Joan as though she could put out her hand and take hold of Angelica's. Or as though she could walk behind Angelica and give her a back rub. It was an unfamiliar feeling because when Angelica was alive there had been many years when she didn't want to be touched by her mother.

Joan was trying to include all of this ambivalence in her painting. Angelica stood straight and tall, but her gestures had an aspect of defiance. Joan had planned to have Angelica's hands in her pockets, but instead she brought them down to her sides and slightly clenched. She had the most difficulty painting Angelica's face. First she tried to make it as beautiful as it had been when Angelica was young, with high cheekbones and smiling eyes. Her brow was peaceful, her nose straight, and her mouth curved into a smile to reflect her eyes. But that face didn't reflect the defiance of her stance or show the exhaustion her depression had caused her. Slowly Joan added wrinkles, blurred the cheekbones, and straightened out the smile a bit so that it looked more wistful than happy.

There was a knock on the door. Joan looked at her watch and realized she'd been painting for hours. Alejandro stood in the doorway and in response to being invited in, he said, "No thank you, I can't stop. But there's an all Bach concert on Saturday at Tanglewood. I wondered if you would like to go with me?"

It took Joan a minute to let go of her images of Angelica in order to actually hear Alejandro's question.

Finally she said, "Yes, I'd like that very much."

"Would you like me to get seats inside or do you prefer being on the lawn?"

Seats inside were expensive. But because of Joan's arthritis she could no longer sit on the ground. "How about we sit on the lawn but we bring folding chairs."

"Good idea. I have just the chairs."

"If you bring the chairs, I'll bring a picnic basket."

"That's a wonderful idea."

"Shall I bring wine?"

'Not for me, I'm afraid. I'm a recovering alcoholic." After a minute he added, "I hope that doesn't frighten you."

"Of course not!"

"Good! I'll see you Saturday."

He turned quickly and headed down the steep stairs. Joan closed the door. Then she slowly turned to stare at her painting from across the room. It looked from there as though Angelica was walking toward her through a fog. She was recognizable, and it looked as though she recognized Joan as well. It felt as though they were seeing each other from either side of the river Styx.

Joan wiped sweaty hair out of her eyes. She was hungry and eager to get out of the apartment. She decided to wash up and treat herself to an expensive sandwich and a latte in the café downstairs.

After eating too much, she was not yet ready to go back upstairs. She walked the half mile to The Globe theater and bought a ticket to the matinee performance of "The Diary of Anne Frank."

Joan had first seen the play on Broadway. The actress playing Anne was only three years older than Joan at the time. And Joan had been overwhelmed by the play and the acting. Now it felt familiar, almost like an old friend. Joan laughed and cried as she watched. When the curtain fell, she was exhausted.

She headed out of the theater into the afternoon sunlight, which felt like a surprise coming after a play set entirely in an indoor claustrophobic attic apartment, and she began to stride toward home to get back to work on the portrait.

When Joan opened the door to her apartment, the portrait stared at her from across the room. Angelica's bone structure was becoming more pronounced by the way her clothes hung on her. Her skin seemed to be more porous. The portrait was becoming much more of a painting than Joan had imagined she could accomplish. Perhaps the greatly talented painter, Angelica, was helping from the other side.

This idea reminded Joan of other times she and Angelica had done things together. When Joan's daughters were teenagers and they moved to New York City, Sarah liked to spend Saturday afternoons at the movies. Angelica and Joan preferred getting on the Fifth Avenue bus and watching the city change as they rode north to "The Cloisters."

"The Cloisters" was a combination of actual cloisters from European monasteries brought over to New York City stone by stone, as well as a museum of paintings and sculptures from the Middle Ages.

Joan loved walking around the cloisters or sitting on a stone wall of a particular cloister to watch the fountain dance at its center. Angelica preferred the paintings. She and Joan would separate into their own worlds for a few hours and then when they came together, they would show each other what had become their favorite thing to look at that day.

Now Joan's favorite thing to look at was the portrait she was creating. She leaned it against the wall next to Angelica's self portrait. She brought her rocking chair into the center of the room and, with a glass of wine in her hand, she settled down to stare at the two paintings.

As she looked back and forth from one to the other, they seemed to merge. Angelica's self portrait no longer looked quite so despairing and Joan's portrait of Angelica no longer looked quite so self confident. From the two portraits Angelica seemed to stare at Joan. She seemed to be smiling.

Joan found herself smiling back. After a while she felt her shoulders relax. Perhaps even now she and her daughter could be friends.

Chapter Twelve

For the trip to Tanglewood, Joan made sushi rolls filled with avocado, grated carrots, and scallions, as well as ham and cheese sandwiches, in case Alejandro found the sushi too fussy.

They arrived around 5:30; people were already establishing their areas on the lawn. Some had brought card tables and were laying out wine glasses, candles and cloth napkins. Many had brought blankets which they laid on the grass and then set their chairs on the blanket. Almost everyone except young children and a few dogs eschewed walking on people's blankets.

Alejandro carried a rolled up blanket and two plastic lawn chairs. Joan carried the picnic basket. They found a less populated area toward the far side of the shed. They were close enough to hear but couldn't see inside.

"These are delicious," Alejandro said, using chopsticks to dip a piece of sushi into a combination of wasabi and soy and then popping it into his mouth.

"I'm impressed by how comfortable you are with chopsticks," Joan said.

"I've eaten a lot of Japanese takeout over the years, while

getting ready for trials."

"I didn't know you were a lawyer as well as a Justice of the Peace."

"I worked with Legal Aid for many years."

"Did you enjoy it?"

"I was more determined to succeed than enjoying it. When I was in college, my grandparents were deported to Mexico. I was born here but my mother died giving birth to me. My grandparents came north to take care of me. When they were deported, I wanted to do what I could to bring them back. I couldn't afford law school but I got a job as a gofer at Legal Aid. After about ten years of night school I finally got my degree."

"Were you able to bring your grandparents back?"

"By that time they had no interest in returning."

"Where were you living?"

"In New York City, on the lower east side."

"I taught kindergarten in that area," Joan told him. "My students were Asian, Hispanic and Black. They had a lot of fun getting to know each other."

"We probably passed each other in the streets many times."

"And what brought you upstate?"

"My wife's family owned a Victorian house in Hudson. When her parents moved to Florida, Beth insisted that we move into their house. She'd loved growing up here and wanted to share the experience with our kids.

"And now, are you considering moving to Mexico?"

"Perhaps. I'm trying to be open to ...." At that moment there was loud applause and they realized that the conductor must have stepped onto the podium. They sat back in their chairs and let Bach put everything to rights. After a while Alejandro reached over and took Joan's hand. The warmth of his hand was surprisingly pleasurable. She was about to pull her hand away as a signal of her independence, but changed her mind. He was just being friendly, maybe because they were both old New Yorkers.

Chapter Thirteen

Joan was delighted a few weeks later when Joe knocked on her door on Sunday evening on his way back to The Academy where he lived and taught during the week. Joan had begun to leave her door unlocked. She felt as though her portrait of Angelica was keeping her company.

Standing in the doorway Joe said, "I bring a message from your daughter. Sarah is eager for you to visit her in the city next weekend."

"Is something special going on?"

"Not that I know of, but sometimes I'm the last to hear. She asked me to call her tonight to say if you're coming. Are you considering getting a phone put in?"

"Yes, I'm considering it, but meanwhile, please tell Sarah that I'd be delighted. Come on in. Would you like a glass of wine, coffee, tea?"

"If you have an open red wine, that sounds perfect. I can only stay a..... Oh my god!"

He stood in front of the painting in silence. Joan had given Angelica a black hat with a wide brim that left part of her face in shadow, and a bright red sheath dress with a wide black leather belt. In one hand Angelica held the straps of a pair of high-heeled silvery sandals, but her feet were bare.

After minutes of staring, Joe said, as though Sarah was in the room with them, "Cover your ears, Sarah, but this crazy sister of yours, was boundlessly beautiful. I can see how she stole your thunder again and again." And then he went back to staring in silence.

After a while he turned toward Joan and sighed before he said, "There's no way you can really show her beauty, but you've gotten enough so that those of us who knew her can remember what she was like."

Joan handed her son-in-law a glass of wine and poured some for herself. She sat down at the table, but he remained standing staring at the painting.

Finally, with a sigh, Joe turned his back on the portrait and joined her. "I wonder how blind people visualize to themselves what people look like. I have a friend; he's been blind since childhood. He's an old man now, a priest. He's the priest I told you about who insisted I contact Sarah when I was in Mexico."

"Father Paul Brown, I remember."

"We've been playing duets."

"Between here and Mexico?"

"He had a stroke in Mexico and was sent to "All Souls", a Jesuit retreat center near Albany. He's gotten back the use of his hands, but he can't walk without help. He used to make a living playing jazz piano before he went to Seminary. Despite being black, he was asked to play all over the city. I want you to meet him."

"I'd like that. Shall we take the train to the city together on Friday?"

"No, I have a Saturday concert at The Academy. I have a feeling Sarah wants to talk with you about women stuff."

"Oh dear. Oh well, another time."

They gave each other bear hugs, and Joe was off.

Chapter Fourteen

The next afternoon Joan went to Treehouse Books to look at Maggie's art books. She arrived just before closing time. As soon as she opened the door, she heard, and then saw, Seamus carefully descending the steep narrow stairs from his office above. Maggie's black and white Newfoundland, Olaf, was right behind Seamus; but Olaf held himself back at every step so he wouldn't push Seamus off balance.

Maggie, looking somewhat like a mother hen, with her comfortably curvy body and her gray hair sliding loose from a barrette, was encouraging her lingering customers toward the front door, although they wandered away from her to show their friends "a book I loved as a child" or one of the "recent arrivals" they'd neglected to examine before. Joan was about to turn around and leave, but Seamus called out to her from the stairs, and Maggie turned to say, "Do stay, Joan. It's been ages since I've seen you."

When Maggie got all her customers quite close to the door, it opened from the outside and Michael came in with Father Paul, who was leaning heavily on a cane.

"Oh, Father, come sit down," Maggie said pointing to the comfortable upholstered chair near her desk. Then realizing that the priest had not seen her, she gently reached out her hand toward him, saying "I'm Maggie, Michael's grandmother, and it's so nice to finally meet you."

Father Paul held his hand out and they shook hands and then Maggie took his elbow and guided him to the chair which was near her desk. She took his hand to touch the chair, which he did feeling its shape before he sat down, saying "Thank you very much."

The customers left quickly, perhaps assuming that a strange religious ritual was about to begin. Maggie locked the door behind them.

Seamus now had the floor under his feet and went over to where the priest sat. "How good to see you, Father."

"It is good to be with you again, Seamus," the priest said, "I enjoyed our conversation."

"I did too, very much." Seamus concurred. "You've just met Maggie, the owner of this wonderful place, and I want to introduce you to a friend of mine. This is Joan Estrada. Her stepson and my niece are married and living in Nicaragua."

"It's very nice to meet you, Joan", Father Paul said, holding out his hand. Joan went quickly toward him and shook it.

"You and I have another connection," she said. "About a decade ago my son-in-law Joe Wilson met you in the Cathedral in Mérida. He'd been living in a cancer clinic there, waiting to die. You convinced him that he needed to tell his wife and children that he was alive. You kept my family together, Father, and I thank you for that with all my heart."

"And now your son-in-law has been visiting me at the retreat house. It was he who found Maggie's grandson, Michael, for me, my terrific chauffeur."

"And now, Maggie," he said, "Michael told me that someone had left some books in braille in front of your door and you wanted to know what they were about."

"Yes indeed. Whoever it was left no note about the books or who they belonged to. I'm wondering if I have blind neighbors that I don't know about."

She handed him a large book, and after quickly running his fingers across the title, and author's name, Paul smiled, and said, "This is an old favorite of mine. It's called "And There was Light" It's by one of the heroes of the French underground during World War II. His name was Jacques Lusseyran. He was blind but he had an uncanny way of knowing who to trust and who to be wary of. His group accomplished a lot before they were finally caught."

Paul sighed for a moment remembering. Then he smiled in the direction of Maggie and said, "Lusseyran was blinded as a child, the way I was. This book was a great help to me describing a young person transitioning from sight to blindness, who then became a hero during the war!"

"When I was in high school," Maggie told him, I volunteered at the Lighthouse in Chicago. I taught spelling which was ironic because I was a poor speller, but I had the words in front of me and my job was to test people on how well they were doing memorizing them."

"What drew you to the Lighthouse?"

"I loved to read. I was afraid that I loved it too much, or counted on it too much, and that God might make me blind because of it. So when my school told us to find a place to volunteer, I chose the Lighthouse so I could see how blind people managed."

"And you ended up owning a bookstore?"

"Yes this store fell from the sky directly into my lap when I needed it most. But now it seems I have a blind neighbor, and I wonder if I should expand. Where do you find books in braille?"

"I've been told there is a lending library for the blind in Albany, but I imagine that it's difficult for people to get to. I wonder if you could become a local branch for them?"

"That would be wonderful! I'll call the schools and see if they know about blind children or parents living locally."

Chapter Fifteen

The next evening just before Vespers, Paul was stopped in the hall of All Souls by Father Gregory who said, "Paul, would you please come to my office for a few minutes at the end of the service?"

During the service Paul tried hard to concentrate on the prayers and the psalms, but he couldn't stop wondering what Father Gregory wanted to talk with him about. Perhaps Father Gregory was angry about Paul's playing the piano. Playing the piano had become a way for Paul to explore the world without leaving the retreat center. It was almost like flying.

"Come in, Paul," Father Gregory called out when Paul knocked on his office door. "There's a letter that arrived for you."

"From Mexico?" Paul asked, hugely relieved.

"No, I'm sorry. This isn't from Mexico. It's from New York City. Come in and sit down." Father Gregory took Paul's elbow and led him to a chair.

"I don't know anyone...." But Paul didn't finish his sentence. His brother, Tom, if he was still alive, lived in New York City.

"When the Bishop asked if you could come here to recuperate from your stroke, he sent your file with you, so that we would know if you were allergic to any medicines and that kind of thing." After a moment Father Gregory continued, "Also so that we would know who to contact if you didn't recover."

"I understand." Paul said feeling weary of it all already.

"The difficulty is that a novice clerk in the office took it into his head, thinking, I'm sure, that he was doing you a favor, to contact the person who was listed as your next of kin. He let your brother know that you were here, which is, I assure you, against our regulations, and I very much apologize for what he's done."

"Oh."

After waiting for Paul to say more, Father Gregory asked, "Would you like me to open the letter and read it to you."

"No," Paul said. "I mean, no thank you." After an awkward pause Paul added, "I think I need to pray about it first."

"Then, here it is," Father Gregory said, as he put the letter into Paul's outstretched hand.

"Thank you," Paul said as he reached for his cane and stood up. Father Gregory guided him by the elbow to his office door. "You know where you are from here?" he asked.

"Yes, I do." Paul said. All he wanted was to get away from the office. He wanted to be invisible, as people were invisible to him. He had no idea where he was. He remembered the feeling of flying when he improvised on the piano which was in a room somewhere nearby. But now he had the feeling of being weighed down by a ball and chain at his wrists and ankles. He longed to simply disappear.

Chapter Sixteen

When Joan arrived at Sarah and Joe's apartment in the city, there was a note scotch-taped to their door. *"Be back in twenty minutes."* Joan didn't know what to do. It was raining hard. The hall where she was standing was ill lit and unwelcoming. Also she needed to sit down. She decided to go back outside to look for a coffee shop. She headed toward the stairs when she heard noises inside the apartment. She turned back and knocked loudly. Sarah opened the door, "Hello Mom, how nice to see you."

"I thought you were out," Joan said, trying not to sound cross and pointing to the note,

"Oh, I was a while ago. I guess I forgot to take that down. Come on in. You're just in time for supper. It's just the two of us, so I figured a salad and soup would be enough."

"Where is everybody?"

"Well Joe can hardly ever get away for weekends. But thank goodness he's making enough money for the rest of us to be here. Sam is on Long Island this weekend meeting his girlfriend's parents for the first time, and Kari's dance teacher has invited the class to spend the weekend at her summer house to attend performances at Jacob's Pillow."

"Oh." Joan tried not to sound as irritated as she felt. "I was hoping to see the kids. I thought that was why you invited me for this weekend."

"No, the truth is the other way around. I asked you to come this weekend because I wanted to be alone with you."

"I wish you'd told me," Joan couldn't stop herself from saying.

"Mom, I know you too well. You wouldn't have come if you knew."

Stopping herself from saying, 'you're right I wouldn't have', Joan asked, "Why do you want to be alone with me?"

"I want to talk woman to woman with you, but first let's have supper. I got some fancy endive and stuffed olives for our salad."

As they ate the small portions of salad, "I need to lose seven pounds," Sarah explained. "I have an audition next week."

Sarah had met Joe when she was in the chorus of The Threepenny Opera and Joe was in the orchestra. Now that their son was studying architecture at Columbia and their daughter was enrolled in the Joffrey Ballet School, Sarah was determined to move back to New York City and make her living as a choreographer. Joe had agreed to make this possible by continuing to teach at The Academy.

Supper seemed to be over before it began. There was no mention of a possible dessert. Joan said, "Shall I do the dishes?" thinking she might sneak a bit more food if she was left alone in the kitchen.

"No Mom, don't you worry about that. I've got something I need to show you. Something really important! This is why I wanted to be alone with you!

It turned out that what she wanted to show Joan was an advertisement in a catalogue for a gadget.

Wear this around your neck
You'll never feel alone again!
In any emergency press the button,
And be connected with your loved ones
In minutes!

When Joan didn't say anything, Sarah announced, "It's waterproof, Mom! You can wear it in the shower."

Joan stared at her daughter. The difference between this being the purpose of her visit, rather than a welcome home with her family, was so ironic that she was speechless.

Her silence geared Sarah up to more dramatic enthusiasm, "Mom, I beg you to do this for my sake! I'm not asking you to do anything showy. You can wear this under your blouse. Nobody need ever know. But I will know, and Joe will know, and your grandchildren will know. We will all know that you are never alone, that no matter how far away from us you are, you can always contact me day or night. Promise me that you will always, always wear this, and you will make me a happy woman! I'll probably be a better choreographer if I don't have to be worrying about you."

Joan wanted to grab Sarah's shoulders and shake her. She was almost trembling with fury at being asked to come all the way to the city to be shown a picture of a gadget. But even more, she wanted to get out of Sarah's apartment and get herself something to eat!

In order to end this conversation she said, "I'll think about it. Right now I think I'll take a stroll. It's such fun to be back in the city."

"But it's raining."

"My jacket is almost waterproof, just like the gadget."

Sarah seemed to have no worries about her mother strolling after dark in the city in the rain. All she said was, "Okay, don't worry about the dishes."

The rain stopped just as Joan closed the door to the apartment building. She began to stroll down Broadway, which was always busy, especially on a Friday night. She loved the energy, the romantic couples kissing on the corners as they waited for the light to change, the children playing tag, running in and out of a large group of adults who were arguing about politics, and the old people, the people her own age, sitting on the benches in the middle of Broadway watching everything happen and remembering earlier days. Joan bought a double chocolate ice cream cone and remembered being young as she combined licking it and strolling.

Joan stayed out as long as possible, wandering into Book Culture on Broadway and strolling the aisles. When the store closed for the night, she headed back to the apartment hoping Sarah was fast asleep.

Chapter Seventeen

The next morning they had coffee and half an English muffin. "I don't know how you stay so thin, Mom," Sarah said, when Joan asked if she had a second English muffin they could share. "I can't have any more, and I'm assuming you don't want a whole one."

"Actually I'd be happy with a whole one, especially if you have regular butter to go on it. I can't tell what this spread is made of."

"Alright if you're really that hungry. Yes, I hide the butter from myself, which," she smiled perhaps for the first time, "is rather a trick to accomplish."

"What are your plans for today?" Joan asked.

"I'm not retired like you. Today I am working on a review of a ballet company that performed in the Village last weekend. I'm hoping I can get it printed in The Village Voice. I never stop working, Mom; I'm trying to help Joe with our expenses. You'll have to entertain yourself. I won't be home for lunch. I'm meeting some women friends. You wouldn't like them. But I'll see you at supper time?

"I think, dear, that I'll go home this evening. It's been lovely to see you, but I've become a sort of country mouse. Also I'm working on a painting and…"

"Yes," Sarah interrupted Joan quickly. "Joe said your apartment smells like a studio because you're using oil paints. He said you did a picture of Angelica. You always did think that she was the beauty. Oh well, even in death she takes precedence. I should be used to that by now."

"Do you remember her self portrait, the one I loaned to The Academy?"

"Yes, a pathetic imitation of Ad Reinhardt."

"Well that's why I tried to do a portrait of her. Her self-portrait was so despairing that I wanted to show a different side of her."

"Mom, she was always the only one of us, I include my children, who really interested you at all."

"She was desperately sick from the time she was seventeen."

"I don't know about desperately sick. She told you she was hearing voices of people who weren't there. It was probably the street drugs she was taking."

"You know she... Oh well, let's let her go, Sarah, both of us. Let's let her go."

"Gladly!" After a minute of silence and deep breathing on both their parts, Sarah said, "Mom, you know I loved her. She was my big sister, and I looked up to her in every way. But she was such a combination of beautiful and pathetic, I felt that she made me disappear even though she didn't try to.

"You, dearest, are beautiful and not at all pathetic. You never disappeared from my heart, nor from my thoughts. I'm so sorry you felt that way. It's true that I was preoccupied by her. I was afraid that she would kill herself unless I was vigilant enough. I'm so sorry."

"Oh, Mom," Sarah put her arms around Joan and kissed her cheek. "I shouldn't have said that. I remember how you took care of Sam those first years so I could keep working."

"I loved doing that. Those were happy years."

Joan kissed Sarah on the cheek, and then stepped back, a little teary eyed. "I think I'll go visit some galleries. Give my love to the kids. I hope to see them next time I come."

"Yes, I'll tell them. They'll be sorry to have missed you. I'm going to say that you arrived on the spur of the moment. I know you don't want me talking about what I'm hoping you'll do."

"As I said last night, I'll think about it."

"The thing is, Mom, I'm trying to be vigilant about you, the way you were vigilant about Angelica. I don't want you to get hurt and not be able to get in touch with me."

"I understand, and I'll ponder it."

"Okay, stay safe and well."

"You too, dear."

Once Joan was out on the sidewalk she sighed and then breathed deeply. There hadn't been enough fresh air in the apartment. She considered finding the nearest subway, but changed her mind. She slung the straps of her overnight bag over her shoulder and started walking downtown.

Her first stop was the Guggenheim, where she checked her bag and took the elevator to the top of the sphere and began slowly to stroll down around and around enjoying immensely watching Calder's hanging mobiles tremble and spin in the air as people blew on them. The bright colors of the mobiles and the airiness of the Guggenheim with its wide empty center giving wonderful long views, as well as close ones, of the art, filled her with joy, erasing into thin air the irritation she'd been carrying as she walked. Finally, she remembered how much she loved Sarah and let the rest go.

She felt lighter and happier when she left the Guggenheim and began the short walk down Fifth Avenue to the Met. There, she wanted to see some old friends, beginning with Rembrandt's "Head of Christ" that she had discovered when she first moved to the city with Angelica and Sarah after Charles died. She'd taken her daughters often to the Met on weekends and suggested that the three of them would each find their favorite painting for the day and then show each other what they'd picked. Often for her it was that particular Rembrandt.

After leaving the Met, she walked on down to the Modern, stopping for some sushi in a hole-in-the-wall Japanese restaurant on Madison Avenue. At the Modern she looked for another old favorite, a sculpture by Louise Nevelson. The back of the sculpture was flat against the wall, but surrounding that was a structure that protruded. It was made of wood and burlap with wire and nails that reached out toward the viewer in a menacing way. But when you stood close to it, almost as though you were face to face with a stranger, and you stared past the nails and the wire, you were staring into a black abyss. Nevelson had created this absolute blackness with black velvet cloth. But in the early days of Joan's visiting it, this sculpture had seemed to be the epitome of abysses. And by staring at it without wincing or blinking, Joan felt she was gaining courage.

Leaving the Modern, Joan walked as fast as she could toward Grand Central Station to catch the express train home.

Chapter Eighteen

Two weeks later, after a Wednesday afternoon painting class, Alejandro knocked on Joan's door again. "Would you consider joining me downstairs at the café for a latte and a piece of apple pie?"

"I would indeed."

Once they were settled at a table by the sunny window with their pie slices and their luxurious coffees, Alejandro said, "My children visited me last week. They decided to all come at the same time. They wanted to choose among Beth's things what to take home. They argued for five days about who should get what. And then yesterday they packed everything up in boxes and drove back and forth to the post office to send home their loot."

"How does your house feel without what they took?"

"The house feels fine. It feels better than fine. The kids found lots of things that were brand new. Beth loved to buy Christmas presents all through the year. It was almost as though they were shopping, but everything was free. Yes it feels very good to have less stuff."

He was silent for a few minutes but then he continued, "In fact, now with the stuff gone I'm ambivalent about selling the house. It feels more like my house, a house where I can stretch out and be comfortable.

"I haven't told the kids of course. They're eager for me to sell it and share the money among them. So eager, in fact, that while they were here the kids contacted a realtor. She came and looked around and said that the house would be worth a good deal of money, but before I could sell it, I would have to empty it completely and move out."

"Are you considering doing that?"

"She told this to me and the kids together. The kids were thrilled and urged the realtor to find me an apartment to move into. The realtor called me this morning. She has three apartments that she wants to show me on Saturday.

After an awkwardly long pause, he said, "Joan, is there any possibility that you would consider coming with me to look at them? It's all moving so fast."

"Sure." Joan said, "It will be interesting to see what's available. Why don't we plan to have supper at my place afterwards so we can discuss what we've seen without the realtor present?"

"Joan, you're a godsend."

The first apartment was on Main Street in Valatie. It was in a two story house that had been divided into studio apartments. All the tenants were from Latin America. One family warned Alejandro in Spanish as he and Joan climbed the stairs, "If you can't fix your own toilet or aren't willing to deal with a rat or two, we suggest you don't move here."

"Truly?" Alejandro answered in Spanish.

"Yes, truly."

"Have you talked with a lawyer?"

"No papers."

"I am a lawyer. Here's my card. Perhaps we can put pressure on your landlord to bring the building up to code."

"He'd just kick us out. Lots of people are looking for apartments. But thank you for your offer."

"At your service."

Alejandro turned to the middle aged realtor who was doing something on her cell phone. "Thank you, but these apartments are too small for me."

The next two apartments were in Carleton. One was right next to the train tracks. As Joan and Alejandro looked around, a train roared by and the floorboards shuddered. The third apartment was directly over a bar and they could imagine the night time noises. "You've been very kind," Alejandro told the realtor, "but we'll need to keep looking." Then he and Joan walked back to her apartment.

Joan realized as they were climbing the stairs that she had forgotten to turn her portrait of Angelica to the wall. When she unlocked her door, there was the portrait staring at them.

Alejandro stood still and stared back. Joan stared as well, trying to see it from his point of view. Finally he turned to Joan and said in Spanish, "I had no idea you were such a painter. Who is this amazing lady?"

Joan let go of the breath she hadn't known she'd been

holding. "She's my older daughter. She took her own life years ago."

Alejandro turned back to the portrait and stared. "Oh my dear, I'm so sorry." Joan wasn't sure which of them he was talking to.

"Would you like some lemonade?" She asked, hoping to break the spell and make him turn away."

"Yes, thank you. Can I help?" When Joan didn't answer he stayed where he was staring at Angelica. Joan put the quiche she'd made into the oven to warm and combined the salad fixings. As she arranged kiwis and clementines in a bowl Alejandro joined her and set the table.

Soon they were eating companionably. Joan told him about Angelica's successful gallery exhibit in Boston, and Sarah's move to New York to become a choreographer. Alejandro told Joan about his daughters wanting to wear their mother's clothes. "One daughter is too large and the other is too thin. They both tried on every dress. My son declared again and again that the dresses would look much better on his wife."

Alejandro insisted on helping Joan wash the dishes. Then he stood again in front of Joan's painting. "How did you become such a good painter?"

"When my husband and his three grown children were in the mountains fighting the Contras, a friend of one of my step daughters, a woman who'd been injured in the war, moved in with me. She'd lost the use of one of her legs. She was a portrait painter from Managua. In exchange for being taken care of, she taught me how to paint. Our neighbors loaned us photographs so she could paint portraits of their loved ones who were somewhere in the mountains."

Alejandro turned his eyes away from the portrait of Angelica and stared for a moment at Joan. "You truly are a godsend!" He put his hands on both her shoulders and quickly kissed her cheek. "I'm off. Thank you for everything." And he slipped out her door before she could say goodbye.

Chapter Nineteen

On Wednesday afternoon Alejandro knocked again. Joan quickly invited him in although she was still smarting a little from his quick departure on Saturday.

"I have a present for you," he said, thrusting forward the large box he was carrying. Joan opened the door wide and he carried the heavy box to the kitchen counter. "It's an espresso machine. You can make lattes with it."

"My goodness!" Joan said, confused by such an expensive present.

"It was on the floor of Beth's closet in its box, brand new. My son wanted to send it home through the mail but it was too heavy. I know you like lattes."

"I do," Joan said, relaxing a little. "You do too."

"Yes, but I already have a machine to make them. And I wanted to thank you for accompanying me on that ridiculous apartment hunting..."

"Alejandro, I enjoyed that; there's..." Joan interrupted him.

"And, I want to ask you for another big favor."

'What's that?"

"The kids are ganging up on me. Supposedly this is just the right time to sell houses. If I wait too long it will be too late. They're saying that If I can't find an apartment, I should live in a retirement community. They've researched for me and found 'just the one.' It's called The Highlands. It has a nursing home as well as independent apartments so I'll be 'all ready for the next stage of life' they tell me."

"How awful! What is the favor?"

"I want to be able to tell them that I've looked at it. It gives me the shivers to think of living in a nursing home, with perhaps a graveyard next door. Would you, dear lady, consider accompanying me to look at this horrendous place?"

Joan was horrified by the sound of it, and said nothing.

"Of course I want you to have the espresso machine either way," Alejandro said with a smile.

"Why don't we try out the machine now while I keep you in suspense." Joan said.

The road leading up the hill to The Highlands was curvy, steep, and narrow, a difficult road, Joan thought, for the elderly to navigate. Perhaps this way they didn't dare go out into the world because they wouldn't be able to get back up the hill again. Once she and Alejandro reached the top, though, the land was as flat as a mesa in Arizona. There was a small pond glimmering in the sunshine in front of a white Victorian mansion with modern wings built on either side.

They parked in the spot allotted for visitors. The walls in the front hall were painted light grey, but there were large framed prints of paintings by Kandinsky and Albers and Picasso hanging on them to mitigate the dreariness of the color. The young woman who sat behind the reception desk noticed Joan looking at the prints, and said, "Aren't they wonderful? We have a new resident whose daughter bought these for us."

Alejandro, after glancing at the prints, turned to the young woman and asked, "Could we look around?"

"Please write your names on this guest list and wear these buttons." She handed them metal buttons that they squeezed over the edges of jackets. "Be sure to bring them back when you sign out as you leave. Otherwise we need to go searching for you in every corner and closet."

After looking around the hall for a minute they both felt the need for air; they went out and wandered along the cement paths, among people being pushed in wheelchairs or hunched over their walkers. "If you don't mind I think I'll sit down." Joan said when she saw an empty bench.

Without saying a word, Alejandro sat down beside her. They looked out to the hills that were aflame with color, as though the trees were putting on the most extravagant showing. Somewhere else the view would have thrilled Joan by the combination of its beauty and its ephemeralness. But sitting on that bench she felt the starkness of the contrast between the ugly cement paths and the beauty of the hills beyond reach.

After a few minutes Alejandro mumbled to himself in

Spanish, "No, this is not where I want to end up."

"I wonder how many family members make it up that hill." Joan mused.

"I don't think I've ever felt so claustrophobic out of doors before," Alejandro said morosely.

"Perhaps we've seen enough?" Joan asked.

"Here give me your button and I'll return them."

They didn't speak while Alejandro drove too fast down the narrow road of hairpin turns. Once they were at the bottom, though, Joan asked, "Do you mind being around people who are drinking?"

"Not at all. It's been a long time for me."

"I've heard of a place I think about half an hour from here where they play jazz on Sunday afternoons. It's supposed to be a Mecca for jazz lovers. Shall we see if we can find it?"

"A mecca for jazz sounds just right. Let's find it."

And they did. The jazz was modern, with lots of dissonance and very little melody. After spending time at The Highlands it felt good to be surrounded by the modern world, hearing the music of now, and not the jazz of generations ago that Joan usually preferred.

Joan ordered a glass of the house red. Alejandro ordered a pot of English tea, and they sat there for a couple of hours, saying nothing, but feeling more and more like friends as the music washed over them.

Chapter Twenty

Joan found herself listening hopefully for a knock on her door on Wednesday afternoons around five o'clock. She told herself not to be ridiculous, and even sometimes went for a walk at this time so she wouldn't be home if Alejandro did happen to knock.

"Actually," she told herself, "He's simply asking me for help. He's a recent widower, with greedy children, and I'm a sort of buffer." But it was her wish that Alejandro would call her that made her decide to put a phone into her apartment.

"Finally, Mom!" Sarah said when Joan called her to give her the number. "You were acting like some sort of pagan."

"Pagan?"

"Yes, like a caveman, trying to turn back the clock. Are you afraid of modern times? Is that why you won't wear the safety phone? You can't imagine how happy I and Joe and the children would be if we knew you were wearing it so that even when we didn't hear from you we'd know that you were fine. I wonder if your stubbornness comes from living too long in Nicaragua which we all know is way behind the times. Or maybe it's the beginning of senility."

For a moment, Joan was speechless. Her mother had spent years in a memory ward and Joan dreaded the possibility of doing the same. Then she sighed deeply, as she remembered that Sarah knew about her fear of inheriting senility and was poking her where she knew it would hurt.

Joan said nothing, taking time to breathe deeply, before she said, "In any case, I now have a phone."

"About time! I gotta go, Mom, I've got an audition," and Sarah hung up before Joan could say goodbye.

The next person Joan called was Alejandro. "What a treat to hear from you, Joan. I was thinking of dropping in on you but I didn't want to disturb you if you were painting. Now I can call first to see if you're free."

"Yes," Joan didn't know what she wanted to say to Alejandro, besides *why don't you come over,* so after an awkwardly long pause, she said just that. "I'm free now. Do you have more apartment possibilities to visit?"

"Oh my dear, you are good. You turn this difficult time for me into pleasure. But no, I've made no more appointments with the realtor. I think she got discouraged by my lack of enthusiasm. But there is a chamber music concert this evening in Hudson Hall. Could I take you out to dinner and then to the concert?"

This was so clearly a date, that Joan demurred for a moment. Was she ready for that? If not, why on earth had she called him? "Yes," she said, "that sounds lovely."

Chapter Twenty-one

Joan's enjoyment in being with Alejandro grew stronger each time they met. She began to feel much younger than her 78 years, more like herself in her twenties when she and her first husband, Charles, hitchhiked through Europe for years taking temporary jobs to support themselves.

She found herself thinking of Charles often as she worked on the portrait of Angelica. When Angelica killed herself in her thirties, Joan had blamed herself for failing as a mother. But she had also blamed Charles for dying when the girls were teenagers. She felt sure that Charles would have known how to stop Angelica's descent into despair.

But as Joan worked on the portrait of Angelica, her decades of pain and guilt about not being able to help her daughter began to soften into realizing the possibility that Angelica had an illness that was beyond her help, and beyond Charles's as well. It felt almost as though Angelica staring out at Joan from the portrait was saying, 'it was nobody's fault.'

She did not mention these thoughts to anyone, but when Seamus told her that he was going to Boston for the weekend, Joan surprised him by asking if she could go with him.

"What would you do in Boston?"

"Well it's really Cambridge, I want to see. I want to see the apartment where Charles and I lived. And I want to visit his grave, and perhaps my parents' graves. I wouldn't be in your way, would I?"

"Well I'm planning to spend the night in the rectory of my friend's church; I don't…"

"That's no problem," Joan interrupted him. My mother was a lifetime member of The College Club of Boston. She left them money in her will to make me a lifetime member as well,"

"My goodness," Seamus mumbled.

"Would I be in your way?" Joan asked again.

"Well we wouldn't be together all the time."

Realizing that he'd rather not have her along, made Joan more determined. "Are you going to see old friends?"

"One old friend, Father Gerald. He's been using my house as a refuge for women fleeing domestic violence. Now his Bishop wants to buy the house.

"Do you want to sell it?"

"I'm not sure. Rose loved the house. She did a lot of the painting and wallpapering herself. After she died, I found I couldn't live there without her. On the other hand, it's hard to imagine selling it.

"Will you see friends from the police department?"

"Probably not. Actually Joan I'd rather not talk about my plans because they're still unsure. If you want to come with me, I'll share with you what I can, but otherwise I'm going to assume you'll be fine on your own."

"That would be perfect, Seamus."

Chapter Twenty-two

Seamus parked near the Carleton Bookstore early the next morning. The street door to the stairs was unlocked, so Seamus slowly climbed the stairs and knocked on Joan's apartment door.

"Come on in. I'm sorry but I'll be ready in a few minutes." As she did the last flurry of preparations she forgot that her portrait of Angelica was facing the room until she heard Seamus exclaim, "My goodness!" After a minute or two he said, "This must be your daughter who died."

"Yes, that's Angelica."

"She's very beautiful, but she looks stubborn and headstrong as well. She must have been a handful."

"She was indeed," Joan said as she gathered up her purse and overnight bag. "I think she found herself a handful as well. I'm ready now."

"Okay." But he stood staring at the portrait. "I hope I haven't been rude."

"Heavens no. She was stubborn and headstrong. I'm glad I've been able to show it in the painting. She also was very hard to help. Finally she took the only way she knew out of her pain. And who could blame her?"

"Not I," he mumbled in his gentlest voice.

"Soon they were heading due east. Joan put on the sunglasses that Seamus had warned her to bring.

"So, Joan, what are your plans in Boston?"

"Angelica was a painter. She had a big show in a gallery on Newbury Street a few months before she died, and I want to visit the gallery and see if there are any unsold paintings.

"What will you do with them?"

"Angelica never made a will, so all her things belong to Sarah and me, but Sarah doesn't want anything of Angelica's. Sarah acts as though being manic depressive might be contagious."

They didn't say anything for a while. Joan enjoyed immensely being driven and being able to stare out the side window rather than being huddled over the steering wheel wondering what the cars whirling around her were about to do.

After quite a long time, Seamus said, "I want to tell you something, Joan, something I haven't told anyone else."

"What's that?"

"I'm falling in love with Maggie."

"Oh, Seamus…" but Joan stopped herself from saying *we all know that; we've known it for years.*

"I don't know what to do about it," he continued. "I'm telling you because you've been married twice. Did you feel you were hurting Charles when you married Oscar? Did you feel you were hurting Sarah?"

"No, I didn't feel I was hurting anyone." Joan said a little curtly, remembering Sarah's sour looks. "I just felt happy. Do you feel Rose would be hurt by your loving Maggie?"

"I wish I knew. I don't see how we ever can know." After that they didn't speak again until they got closer to Boston.

"Do you visit Charles's grave when you're in Boston?" Seamus asked.

"I used to. I haven't been in Boston for a while."

"And Oscar's grave in Nicaragua?"

"No, I don't know where that is. Oscar and his daughters died during the war. They are buried somewhere in the mountains. After the war I sometimes hiked up into the mountains and found a boulder or a fallen tree to sit on and think about them."

"Did they seem to talk to you?"

"No, but it was beautiful up there, lots of trees and boulders and a stream. It had been a place of killing, but now it seems a place of peace. I felt that Oscar and the girls were at peace, and I should concentrate on being helpful to Juan, the only survivor of the family."

"When you fell in love with Oscar, did you feel you were loving Charles less?"

"By the time I fell in love with Oscar, Charles had been dead for decades."

"Even so."

"Does the Church say you shouldn't love more than once?"

"No, it doesn't. But the thing is I promised Rose. I told her, just before she slipped away, that I would never love anyone else. That's one of the things I found myself talking about with Father Paul. I couldn't stop talking about her, how much I loved her and missed her, and how awful I felt about her brother James being killed after I'd convinced him to join the police.

"Father Paul suggested I try to talk to Rose. 'Give yourself a place, and a time, say your piece, and then listen,' he told me."

"Listen?" Joan asked.

"'Yes, listen and see what happens.'"

"Listen to what?" Joan asked.

"I didn't have a chance to ask him. A bell began tolling in the building. A nun ran over to where we were sitting under an oak tree. With a quick "I'm sorry" she turned Father Paul's wheelchair around and rushed him back to the retreat center. I didn't have a chance to even thank him."

Chapter Twenty-three

Joan had not visited the College Club since her mother's death. The eliteness of the place, which made her mother so comfortable, was an anathema to Joan. She was welcomed politely, and shown to her room with its four poster bed and velvet love seat as well as an old fashioned wooden desk. Joan dropped her backpack on the bed, and headed outside to Commonwealth Avenue.

She took a subway to Porter Square and walked a few blocks north on Mass Ave until she got to the front door of the building where she and Charles had lived. During their years of travels and temporary jobs they had become fluent in Italian, German, and French. When they decided to settle in Cambridge, Charles found a job in publishing and Joan became a stay-at-home mom with their two daughters.

The downstairs door of the building was unlocked, and for a moment Joan considered climbing the stairs to the second floor and asking the tenant if she could look around for a moment.

When she decided not to do that, she turned her back on the building and faced Mass Ave. The sun suddenly blinded her. She shut her eyes tight, feeling the sun warm her face, almost like a furnace. She heard the Mass Avenue Bus rumbling towards her. She heard the desperate honks, the crash, and the screams! But then, she heard what she had never heard before. Charles was saying into her ear, "*I'm okay; you and the girls will be fine, and I'm okay.*"

But we aren't fine, Joan silently told him. *I failed Angelica!*

"That's not how she sees it", Charles said directly into her ear.

A cloud came between her and the sun. She opened her eyes. The bus, the body lying on the road, and the shouting onlookers all disappeared. What was left was slow-moving traffic; on the other side of the road golden-hued trees swayed in the autumn briskness.

Feeling dazed, Joan found a Bodega on a side street and bought herself a grilled cheese sandwich and a bottle of ginger ale. She took them to Arlington Cemetery and sat on a bench to eat her lunch. A lot had happened at the cemetery since she and the girls had buried Charles. As she looked around she saw that it might take hours before she could locate Charles's grave. *But there's no need,* she realized. *He's sitting on this bench next to me. And he is okay!*

Feeling lighter and freer and enjoying the warm sun beating down on everything, Joan left the cemetery without exploring the headstones. She took the subway into Boston to visit the gallery that had represented Angelica. The young clerk looked Angelica up on her computer and told Joan that the only painting they hadn't sold at her last show was the self-portrait that they had sent to her. "Of course we only list the paintings we represent. She may be represented by a gallery somewhere else, such as in New York."

"That's true," Joan said, trying to remember the name of a gallery in New York that Angelica might have mentioned.

From Newbury Street she slowly walked back to the College Club. The gathering darkness penetrated by lights suddenly appearing in the many windows made her feel like Inspector Adam Grant in Josephine Tey's novels. Life felt like a mystery to be explored day by day. She stopped at a Latino grocery store and bought three tamales and a fried plantain to take back to the club.

After eating supper in her room, she went downstairs to the lobby to call Alejandro from the phone booth.

"Joan dear, how lovely to hear your voice. Are you enjoying yourself? Are you going to the Boston Symphony tonight? They're doing a Chopin you like."

"I think I'll stay in tonight. I've been out all day."

"Ah, too bad. I wish I were there to encourage you."

"I wish you were." After she said that, Joan realized it was true. She would have loved to explore Boston with Alejandro.

"Do you have a new perspective on your portrait of Charles?" Alejandro asked next.

"I think I'm going to give up working on it."

"Why's that?"

"Charles was very young when he died. I think if I were able to make him look the way he looked then, I would be putting him at a great distance from me, almost a lifetime apart. I have no idea what he would look like now. I want to nurture my image of his growing old along with me but on the other side of the river."

"Ah yes, the river Styx that you've told me about. Joan, you are a wonderful painter with words as well as with colors."

"Thank you, that's a lovely thing to say. Have you been apartment hunting?"

"No, I haven't heard back from the realtor. The advertisements in the paper make the apartments sound much better than being on that God-awful hill we visited, but they're all outside of my budget. The kids are going to have to wait a while."

At that moment someone knocked on the door of the phone booth. "I have to go" Joan told Alejandro. "I'll call you from home tomorrow."

"I look forward to it my dear." And they hung up.

When the phone booth was free again, Joan called Sarah to ask if she knew which gallery in New York had represented Angelica.

"Of course not Mom. That was ages ago. I bet you'll not find one person in all of New York City who would remember her name."

Chapter Twenty-four

After Seamus let Joan off at the College Club, he drove to the Church Rectory near his old house, and parked.

It felt both comfortable and strange to be walking the streets of Boston again. He made a detour around the neighborhood where he'd worked and finally came to the cemetery where Rose and her brother James were buried, and where a plot awaited him on the other side of Rose.

He stood and stared down at their flat stones. "Died to Save Strangers" was what Rose had chosen for James's stone. "Teaching by Loving" was what Caitlin and Seamus had chosen for Rose's stone.

After standing and staring at their gravestones for a few minutes, Seamus sat down on a bench a few yards away. James's death, when he was still in his twenties, had devastated Rose and she had begged Seamus to ask for a desk job in the police department.

Sitting on the bench Seamus now silently told her, *I couldn't sit behind a desk while my friends risked their lives. Also, I loved my work. I felt I was doing what God wanted me to do.*

Then he went on to tell her, his words not leaving his lips but echoing in his brain, *Gerald's Bishop wants to buy our house. Gerald has been using it to hide women and children who are fleeing their batterers. The Bishop wants to make it an official sanctuary but the house would need certain changes for that, so he wants to buy it. You made the house so beautiful. What would you think of letting the Church have it as a refuge?*

And then Seamus stopped talking. He began to listen as Father Paul had suggested.

Birds called to each other; a bus's brakes squeaked on an unseen street; and two teenage boys, also unseen, shouted epithets at each other. After that nothing. Seamus listened intently into that brief nothingness and felt for a minute that perhaps he had been heard by Rose. Almost immediately a car, dragging its muffler, pulled into the cemetery parking area.

After a hamburger and a beer in a familiar pub, Seamus took a bus back to the Church where he had parked his car and then walked a block to his old house. He knocked lightly but a nun immediately opened the front door. When Seamus introduced himself, she said, "Father Gerald said you might be coming. You're most welcome. I'm sorry to say there's nobody at home right now. The children are at school and the moms are at the community center. Can I be of service to you in any way?"

"Thank you sister. I'd just like to come in for a moment and look around."

"You do that then. I can't let you go upstairs though. Many of our mothers are hiding from men who've mistreated them. Father Gerald and the doctor are the only gentlemen who are allowed upstairs."

She then headed for the stairs herself, as she said, "I'm going to get things ready for when everyone comes back." Seamus appreciated her tact in leaving him alone. He stepped into the living room.

The walls were covered with drawings and watercolors. There were large pages of children's hand prints in different colors. There were paintings of square houses with stick families in front of them holding hands. There was a drawing of a man wearing mufti and carrying a rifle. Above the man's head was the title: "My Dad." Seamus stared at that drawing for a long time, wondering if the dad was being remembered as a hero in the war or if he had pointed a rifle at the child and his mother before they fled.

The sofas and chairs were crowded with stuffed animals and dolls. The floor was a highway for miniature cars and trucks as well as toddler- size tricycles. Seamus moved a Pooh Bear to one side of a love seat so he could sit down. His house was once again overflowing with the energy of children, but this time it was children in crisis.

When he heard the nun walking toward the stairs, he got up from the love seat as quickly as possible; he called out his thanks toward the second floor and slipped out the front door. When the door clicked shut behind him, Seamus realized he was still holding the Pooh Bear who seemed to be blinking in the sunlight.

Sighing, half wanting to hug the bear to his own chest, he

knocked on the door again. When the nun opened the door, he thrust the bear toward her with an embarrassed smile. She greeted it warmly as though it were a child returning from school. No words needed to be said.

That night Seamus and Gerald shared a supper of Chinese takeout in the rectory kitchen. Seamus stretched his leg with the prosthesis under the wooden kitchen table with a sigh. He hadn't walked so far since he'd lost his foot years before. He felt wonderfully relaxed and happy. He and Gerald had been friends for decades. They talked about politics, the Patriots, and car repair.

Father Gerald left for early Mass before Seamus woke up. Seamus left him a thank you note and headed out into the street to find breakfast. The coffee house where he and Rose used to go was still in business. Seamus felt welcomed by the familiarity of it as he slid into a booth. He was reaching for the menu when he heard Rose say distinctly, "For goodness sake, sell the house and marry the lady!"

Chapter Twenty-five

Maggie put the heavy books in braille that had appeared on her doorstep on the Recent Arrivals table. One of them, "And There was Light" she knew all about. After hearing Father Paul describe it, she had found a copy in regular print at the library and read it in a day. The blind author was a hero of the French Underground during World War II, and he'd written an exciting page-turner memoir. The second book was a biography of Louis Braille. She had found a biography of Braille in regular print and became fascinated by the story. Louis Braille was blind when at the age of fifteen he designed an alphabet and notation system for music and mathematics in 1824, which has been used ever since by blind people all over the world. Helen Keller, both blind and deaf, said that the blind were as indebted to Louis Braille as mankind is to Gutenberg and his printing press.

After Father Paul had told her about the books she'd been given, Maggie called the NYS library in Albany that loaned out books in braille. She described where Treehouse Books was and explained, "I thought you might want to make me a branch of your library since I have at least one blind neighbor. Their immediate response was to make sure the books had not been borrowed from them. Then they explained that they would rather use local libraries to promote their books.

When she hung up, Maggie felt embarrassed. Why had she imagined that they would want her to loan out books locally? She had imagined Michael loaning Father Paul a different book each week, and whoever else came into the store being happy to find local access to books in braille.

Meanwhile she decided she would keep the two books in braille on her recent arrivals table, although they took up a lot of space. And she would offer to lend them to Father Paul.

The glory of autumn was over. The sky was layer upon layer of grey. The brilliantly colored leaves were now brown and crinkly under foot as Maggie and Olaf took their afternoon walk. Treehouse Books was going through a quiet time, the lull before the storm that would begin the day after Thanksgiving when crowds would come in to find 'just the right' second hand book as a thoughtful and inexpensive gift.

When she and Olaf got back from their walk, Maggie called the All Souls Retreat House and asked to speak with Father Paul. She invited him for Thanksgiving, and he sounded delighted. The sound of his pleasure erased her embarrassment about the call to the library!

Chapter Twenty-six

Seamus was the first person to arrive early on Thanksgiving afternoon. He brought two bottles of wine from The Urban Grape in Boston. "This was Rose's favorite store for wine."

Maggie noticed the tone of what he was saying rather than the words. In the past when Seamus spoke of Rose he seemed to put a moat around himself and her. But now he was sharing Rose's opinion as if that might influence Maggie.

Then Michael arrived with Father Paul, who handed Maggie a bag of coffee beans grown in a monastery in El Salvador. "Thank you, I love good coffee," she told him. With one hand now free, Father Paul unbuttoned his coat. Michael quickly took it from him, as Maggie said, "I want to show you around, Father Paul." She took Father Paul's hand that wasn't holding his cane and led him around the living room. She let him feel the table and chairs where they would eat, and the sofa, and the upholstered chairs.

Sitting around the table as they feasted Maggie felt both fascinated as well as a little guilty as she blatantly stared at

Father Paul. He was thin; his loose clothes showed he'd lost weight. His eyes looked normal except that they focused on nothing. His head turned in the direction of whoever was speaking. Perhaps he could hear what people were saying more clearly if he faced them. His expression was gentle and he often smiled when people spoke to him, but Maggie felt that there was the strength of iron behind his gentleness.

They talked about Thanksgivings of their past.

Father Paul described his memory of the Macy's Thanksgiving Day Parade. He had been taken before he was blind and had been flabbergasted by the huge animals that seemed almost as high as the buildings.

Michael talked about Diwali in India. "People light every possible lamp. It's to celebrate the victory of light over darkness. But it also involves a feast."

Seamus told about the first Thanksgiving after he and Rose had adopted Caitlin. "She was just big enough to sit in a high chair and she kept the whole table laughing with her antics. It was the beginning of her career in theater."

Again Maggie felt a new openness in Seamus describing his life with Rose. Maggie told them about her Thanksgiving four years before. "It was the year Michael came to live with me. I'd invited Seamus and a neighbor with teenagers. Just as we were about to dig into the meal, the electricity went off! My neighbors and I sat in awkward silence while Michael and Seamus within minutes got a fire going in the wood stove, and candles on the table. And so we ate, and said what we were grateful for as though nothing had interrupted us." She beamed at them both now.

After dinner they settled on the upholstered chairs and the sofa and drank the strong delicious coffee from the beans Father Paul had brought.

"Where did you grow up, Father Paul?" Maggie asked.

"I grew up in Harlem."

"What was it like then?"

"I remember mostly the sounds. The sights have become somewhat blurred. I remember hearing friendly conversations shouted over my head by people leaning out over their window sills on opposite sides of the street. I remember the sound of cards being slapped down and the chuckles and friendly curses from the men playing cards on a makeshift table brought out on the sidewalk. In the streets my friends played stick ball and made loud hoots of derision at the cars that were trying to get by them."

As Father Paul said those words, the phone rang. Maggie got up to answer it. After a minute of hearing excited Spanish, she simply handed the phone to Seamus. After he listened for a minute or two, Seamus said a few words in Spanish and hung up. "I am sorry, Maggie, but I need to move a family out of their apartment before it gets too dark. Michael, could you possibly help me?"

"On Thanksgiving?" Maggie asked in annoyance.

"It's a long story," Seamus said, as he and Michael stood

up. "I'll be back as soon as I can, Father, to drive you home," Michael said.

"I will drive Father home," Maggie said decisively.

Chapter Twenty-seven

After Seamus and Michael left, Father Paul and Maggie sat in silence for a few minutes. Maggie was surprised by how comfortable she felt. Perhaps the wine they'd shared helped. Or perhaps it was the delicious coffee.

Maggie was about to tell him how much she had enjoyed reading "And There Was Light", but Father Paul, not knowing that she'd opened her mouth to speak, said, "I have a brother. He's three years older than me. Tom was almost ten when I was hit by a car and blinded."

"Was he with you when it happened?" Maggie asked.

"Yes, he was supposed to be taking care of me. He and his friends were playing stickball in the street. I ran into the street after a fly ball."

Maggie didn't know what to say, so she said nothing.

"I'm thinking of him now because he sent me a letter. I hadn't heard from him in more than forty years."

"Why was that?"

"After my ordination I was sent to Mérida in Mexico. My parents and Tom couldn't understand why I would go somewhere just because I was told to by the Bishop. They had assumed I would stay on in Harlem. Then, when my parents died in an accident, the Bishop in Mérida was ill and asked me not to leave for the funeral. When I telephoned home to explain, Tom called me everything under the sun and told me never to call or write to him again."

After a long silence, Maggie asked, "And now?".

"And now a letter has come from him. The retreat house wrote him about my stroke."

For a while they continued to sit in companionable silence. Then Maggie asked, "Was his letter friendly?"

"I don't know," Father Paul told her. "I haven't read it yet.

"The thing is," he continued after a few minutes, "when we were young I was the albatross wrapped round Tom's neck. When I was blind our parents said to Tom maybe thirty times a day, 'Take care of your brother. Don't let your brother out of your sight.'

"Tom's method of taking care of me was to sit me on a stoop and say 'Don't move from here or I'll knock your head off.' Then he would play stick ball with his friends while I sat tight and listened to their game, and to the conversations around me, and to the people walking past. Before I was blind I had no idea about the range of sounds one could listen to.

"At other times I was the excuse Tom used when he wanted to avoid something. He would grab the back of my tee shirt and push me down the street in front of him like a shield, calling over his shoulder, "Can't do that now. I've got to take care of the kid."

"Did you get angry?"

"I both hated how he was treating me and felt a desperate

need for his protection, especially that first year when the pitch black darkness left me dazed."

"What about your parents?"

"They both worked full time. I was Tom's responsibility from when we got out of school until six o'clock. Tom complained bitterly that I was destroying his social life. 'Not just my social life, but my actual life.' I can still hear him saying it."

"Do you think he'll say something like that in his letter?"

"It could be that he still thinks of me as his burden to bear."

"After a long silence Maggie asked, "Do you want me to read the letter to you?"

"Yes," Father Paul said with a sigh. "I would appreciate that." He took a much folded envelope out of his pocket and handed it to her.

Paul,

It's time we get together. Janie is an ER nurse and knows all about strokes. The kids have moved out so you can have your old room. I'm not able to work because of a bum knee so I'll enjoy your company. Come home, Paul, it's time.

Tom

Neither of them said anything for a long time. At first the silence felt awkward, but after a while, Maggie could feel her body relax and she leaned back on the comfortable sofa.

Finally Father Paul said, "You're very kind to offer to drive me back to All Souls. Would you be able to go for a walk with me first? I'd like to stretch my legs and get a bit of air."

"Me too," said Maggie, "I'll get our coats."

Once they were out on the dirt road, which was disappearing as falling snow and early winter darkness took over, they hooked elbows and held each other up as they walked. As the snow became heavier and neither of them could see where they were going, Father Paul and Maggie began to belt out "Good King Wenceslas" into the listening silence.

Chapter Twenty-eight

"I'm going to give you an early Christmas present, Father Paul," his doctor said, sounding proud of herself. "I'm going to give you the name and the phone number of the best stroke specialist in New York City. He has a long waiting list, but I telephoned him. I described your condition and I made it sound interesting enough, because of course it is interesting, that he agreed to see you. Here it is." She handed him a slip of paper. "Show this to that driver of yours and get on the phone and make an appointment. Do you have a place to stay in the city?"

Two Weeks Later

The downstairs door was unlocked. Paul climbed two flights of stairs and knocked on the far door on the third floor. It was Janie who asked who was there and then opened the door. Without a word she put her arms around him and held him in a tight embrace as though to squeeze out any of the difficulties that had ever arisen between them.

Tom then hugged him as well. Unlike Janie's, Tom's heavy handed hug felt somewhat like a revenge for old hurts.

Janie guided him into the kitchen saying, I made your old

favorites although you've probably grown out of them. We're having franks and beans and chocolate pie for dessert.

"I don't think one can grow out of liking those," Paul said. "I'll just wash up." He found that moving around the apartment, the apartment he'd grown up in, his feet didn't need his head to tell them where to go.

As they ate, they talked about the children and grandchildren who were living in Chicago and Georgia. Janie enjoyed visiting them, but Tom said his bum knee was making even seeing his kids hard to do. They asked Paul about his health and Tom declared, "We'll go with you tomorrow. I'll stay in the waiting room, but you'll need Janie in there with you to ask the right questions and to translate if the doctor uses too much Latin.

Chapter Twenty-nine

After having been poked and prodded, in New York City, Paul was eager to hear what his Albany doctor, who had sent him on this uncomfortable journey, had to tell him about the results. He paced the claustrophobic examining room now warily waiting for her entrance. She was keeping him waiting for so long that Paul wondered if she was postponing bad news.

"The results are both good and bad," she announced, as she finally entered the room.

"Good morning, doctor" Paul said, as he heard her make herself comfortable on her stool. He reached around until he felt the patient's chair and carefully lowered himself into it.

"You say things are good and ..."

"Yes I did" she interrupted him sharply. "Your numbers don't look too bad."

She stopped there. Paul assumed that she was gazing into her computer as though she were reading a thriller novel that she couldn't look up from. Finally she said, "Yes, they're not too bad. After all, at your age one shouldn't expect ..."

"Is that the good news?" Paul interrupted her, finally losing his patience.

"Yes, that's the good news. You're a lucky man to have such a strong constitution. I know many much younger men with worse numbers."

Then she was silent again.

Paul could wait no longer and asked, "And the bad news?"

"The bad news is that despite all the tests we have not been able to find the cause of your first stroke. Therefore there is nothing we can do to prevent another stroke from occurring. You could experience another stroke, perhaps a more lethal one, tomorrow or next year. I'm not able to predict how soon it will happen, but I believe it is important that you understand, as you plan the rest of your life, that it is very likely that you will experience more strokes.

"But as for this stroke, we've done all we can to help you recover, and so there is no need for me to see you again, until…. I wish you well."

That evening, back at the retreat center, Father Gregory asked if Paul would meet with him in his office. As soon as they were both seated. Father Gregory said, "I don't know if you are aware that all your medical records are automatically shared with our office while you are our guest."

"Yes, Father, I assumed that."

"The present report says the doctors have done all they can for you. This means that All Souls can no longer have you here as a medical emergency guest. I don't mean to rush you into a decision, but if you are to stay on here, it would be as a long term resident, and we would expect you to stay on the premises except for medical emergencies."

Paul felt as though he was hearing the door of a jail cell slam shut. They sat in silence for a few minutes before Father Gregory continued, "Now, it seems to me that you are too well for that, and that you would quickly become restless. What do you think?"

Paul sat back in his chair, confused and feeling battered. He took three deep breaths letting Father Gregory wait for his answer. Finally, with the third breath, he realized that Father Gregory was talking about money.

Father Gregory himself must have realized how unclear he'd been. For now he said, "Our resources are stretched, you see, and we need to be exact in our accounting."

"Can you give me until tomorrow to think this over?" Paul asked, as he felt on the floor for his cane.

"Yes indeed, Paul, I can give you to the end of this week."

Paul stopped in his room to grab and put on his coat, hat and scarf, and then he pushed open a side door and went out into the night to sit on a bench near the back entrance to the kitchen and began to pray.

What he had been longing for, and expecting all these months of being away, was to return to the Cathedral in Mérida. But now he could not ask the Bishop, who was somewhat frail in health, to take him on again, facing the probability of another stroke.

He could stay on at the retreat center as a long term resident. But, Father Gregory's description of what would be expected of him made that sound like being imprisoned for the rest of his life.

Tom's wife was a nurse who knew all about strokes. How terribly ironic it would be if having been a burden to Tom as a boy, he would be a burden to Tom's wife as an old man.

Paul prayed for a way out of the need to return to Tom's care, but he could find no alternative.

Finally, shivering from the cold, Paul went inside to make a long distance call to the Cathedral in Mérida. His friend, Jorge, answered the phone and was at first thrilled to hear Paul's voice. But after Paul told him of his situation and his decision, Jorge did his best to change Paul's mind. "Let me talk with the Bishop, dear friend. We need you here."

"The doctor said I could have another stroke as soon as tomorrow. I can't ask the Bishop to take me on. And it is possible, Jorge, that this is what I'm being asked to do. Perhaps my brother and I are being given a chance to heal from what happened in the past."

"May God bless you, Paul, in all that you do. I will pray for you daily."

"Bless you, Jorge, and thank you."

Chapter Thirty

Maggie was saying goodbye to lingering customers and attempting to close the door of the bookstore, when Michael slipped in before the door was quite shut. He panted as though he'd been running and had no breath left, but he managed to say, "He's not coming back!"

"What?" Maggie asked, thinking that Michael was prophesying about one of the customers who had just left.

"He's not coming back! He's going to live in the city. He's not coming back here. Ever!"

"Father Paul?"

"Of course Father Paul."

"Oh, Michael! Come sit and tell me about it." The wood stove was going strong near her desk and there was a comfortable upholstered chair facing it. Before sitting down, Michael put another log in the stove. Maggie pulled her chair away from her desk so she could face him.

They were both silent for a while. Maggie saw that Michael was trying to force tears down his throat. Finally, she asked, "Did Father Paul tell you why he was moving to the city for good?"

"He's not going to get better. That's what the doctor told

him. Imagine telling someone that he's not ever going to get better!"

"Do you mean that he's dying?" Maggie wished she hadn't said that even before the words were out of her mouth.

"He doesn't know. He said it's like walking in the woods during a thunderstorm and not knowing if the wind will bring a tree crashing down."

Maggie thought of saying *isn't that true for all of us?* but instead she asked, "What is it about Father Paul that makes him so important in your life?"

"He always needs help because he can't see, but he has no self pity, no resignation, no embarrassment. He accepts everything about himself. In that way he's amazingly strong!"

"Who's amazingly strong?" Seamus was slowly coming down the steep stairs carefully holding on to the banister with Olaf patiently plodding behind him. Sometimes Seamus urged Olaf to go down the stairs in front of him but Olaf always preferred to let Seamus lead even though it was slow going.

"Father Paul." Michael called up to Seamus.

"Yes, indeed. Strong and generous. Thank you Michael for introducing him into my life."

"He's moving, Seamus. He's moving to New York."

"Oh. Well then let's go visit him there."

At that, Michael got up quickly and ran to the foot of the stairs saying, "Can we?"

"Of course we can."

Michael stood taller and straighter, and turned toward Maggie with a vibrancy in his expression that almost brought Maggie to tears. Instead of crying she said, "How about meatloaf for supper? Seamus, will you join us? Michael taught me how to make a special meatloaf with mushroom sauce."

"That sounds wonderful."

"I'll go get it started. I know where..." Michael said, out the door before he finished his sentence.

Michael's meatloaf was delicious. "I can't tell you how grateful I am that you're such a good cook," Maggie said as they sat back in their chairs sated. Michael didn't say, as he well could have, *Your cooking's so bad Grandma, that I had to be.* Instead, he said, "Dad did all the cooking in India."

"Well," Seamus said, "I'm glad you're bringing your abilities to American food. That was outstanding!" Then he turned to Maggie to ask, "Did Michael tell you about our new project?"

"No."

"People have been telling us about their difficult trips across the borders in Texas and Arizona. They walk nonstop for days and nights, carrying children, and food and water which they often run out of. The hardest thing is when one of them gets ill. The coyote who is guiding them, refuses to stop for any reason. Sometimes they come upon plastic jugs of water that people have hung on posts for them..."

"But sometimes those jugs have bullet holes in them and

the water has drained out into the sand," Michael interrupted. "Seamus got the idea of asking those who could, to write about their experiences. And those who couldn't write, to dictate their stories to him. Then, Seamus and I will translate their stories into English and maybe make a bilingual booklet. That way the people here could send the booklet to their families back home to tell them what the journey is really like."

"We'd keep everything anonymous of course," Seamus interjected and we'd only do it with the permission of the story teller."

"And then the booklet would also become the text to teach people how to read English!"

"That was Michael's idea. I can't think of a better way to learn a language as an adult than to read things that you yourself have written."

"They could write about other things as well," Michael continued, "for example what their life is like here. Seamus introduced me to two old men who don't know how to read and write, not even their names. They put an 'X' when someone asks for their signature. Both of them have been working here a long time sending money to their families in Mexico. And with that money their children and grandchildren are going to school and college. One of the children is studying to be an architect! These men never see their families because coming north across the border is so dangerous. Instead they work in Texas in the winter and up here in the summer and they're happy and proud knowing that their work is ensuring that their families are eating well and being educated."

Maggie stared at the two men she loved so much. It's enough to love them, she realized. *I've no need to be loved by them in return*, she told herself. *My cup is overflowing.*

Chapter Thirty-one

Michael picked Father Paul up at All Souls and drove him to the train station in Carleton. When they arrived, Michael opened Father Paul's door, and handed him his cane. Every familiar gesture felt strange to them both because it might be the last time it happened. Father Paul felt for Michael's shoulders so he could face him head on. "I'm not sure I would have gotten this well without your help." Father Paul told him.

"Me too," Michael said.

"You're going to be a leader in whatever field you decide to focus on."

"Thank you, Father. God bless." Father Paul heard the tears in Michael's voice as he handed him his suitcase, got back in the car and drove quickly away.

When it was much too late Paul realized he hadn't blessed Michael, hadn't prayed over him, hadn't done anything, but prophesied.

When Paul knocked on the apartment door, Tom opened it with a flourish, "Welcome home, Bro. Here give me your suitcase. I've put you in the room you and I shared growing up. Do you need a hand or do you remember your way around?"

"I remember the rooms but I'll keep my cane because I don't know where the furniture is."

"Shall I help you unpack?"

"It's better if I do that on my own. That way I'll remember where I put things."

"Okay, I'll finish supper. We're having your old favorite, 'pigs in a blanket'. Janie's at the hospital until eleven so it's just the two of us. I hope you still like Budweiser."

"A cold 'Bud' sounds like a treat," Paul said although he hadn't had a beer in decades.

"Good. Come into the kitchen when you're ready."

Chapter Thirty-two

The next time Sarah asked Joan to come to see her in New York for a weekend, Joan asked if the children would be home. "Yes, Mom, Kari is in a dance recital. That's why we're inviting you. She is eager to have you see her. Sam will be here as well. Even Joe is getting away from The Academy for a weekend. He told me to tell you he'd be glad to bring you with him on the train.

Joan and her son-in-law were old friends. They both had spent years in Nicaragua, and now as they traveled toward the city on the train they spoke in Spanish. Joe confided "The Academy has offered to make me a resident musician which would mean I could spend more time in the city, but the stipend wouldn't be enough to cover Sarah's rent."

"I think you've been hugely generous to continue at The Academy so Sarah can take dance lessons and audition for jobs. You are the one who should be in the city. You could have a career there, while Sarah can only dream of becoming a choreographer."

"I want to give her the chance to try. Teaching at The Academy is not that bad. I'm composing a quartet for my advanced students. Living on my own during the week gives me more time to compose, though of course I miss everyone."

When Joe opened his apartment door with his key, Sarah was standing in the hall waiting for them. "So nice to see you, Mom. Hello Joe dear. Joe, would you please open a white wine to let it breathe?" Then she said in a softer voice as she helped Joan off with her coat, "That's a lovely dress, Mom. If you like, I'll lend you my suede coat to go with it. You're going to be proud of Kari. I went to the dress rehearsal. She's outstanding. Do you remember how well I danced before I got pregnant with her? I like to think that the energy and ability I had flowed into her body."

That night Joan was awed and thrilled watching Kari perform her solo. She was dancing to a piece that Joe had composed for her! Until now she'd been rehearsing with the tape he'd made. But this night, Joe stood in the wings and accompanied her. Between them they created an experience of drama and beauty that made the audience give them a standing ovation!

The next morning over breakfast, Joan's grandson, Sam, told her, "I'm going to be interning with Caples Jefferson Architects this summer. Would you like to see one of their buildings?"

"I'd like that a lot," Joan told him.

They took the subway to the Corona neighborhood in Queens where Louis Armstrong and his wife had lived. As they walked toward it, Sam explained, as he pointed toward a modest two story brick building, "Right there is where Louis Armstrong and his wife lived for many years. After his death his widow turned their house into a museum. Right across the street from the house the CJA built the Louis Armstrong Center. What do you think?"

Joan stared at the beautiful curves of the building, that contrasted with, but did not overwhelm, the two story simple houses on either side. "I think it's terrific. I love those slow moving curves. They make the building look like Armstrong's music itself. I'm so glad you will be interning with them, and who knows what will happen after that?"

"Yes, I'm really hoping they will hire me in the long run. Do you want to see one of my favorite new buildings? It's by Zaha Hadid."

"Sure," Joan said, loving being part of what mattered to Sam.

They took the subway back into Manhattan. On 34th Street they climbed up the stairs to the High Line, a walkway 30 feet above the streets, with plants and benches, almost like a path in Central Park, but with the amazing perspective of being so high. "I love this," Joan told him. "It feels magical to be walking comfortably among the upper stories of buildings, and at the same time to be surrounded by greenery."

Suddenly the building they were looking for appeared like

two huge waves rising up beside them and reaching for the sky. They stood and stared at the wonder of it. Then they descended the stairs to 28th Street. "From here it seems to be made of layer upon layer of thin waves of glass glittering in every direction," Joan said. Sam led her inside where they explored the public areas. "I feel as though I'm diving and floating and diving again through the waves."

They were home in time for tea. Sarah was at an audition, but Joe and Kari had made brownies. Joan was filled with quiet joy at seeing how vigorous, creative and independent her grandchildren were. When they told her they were going to a supper party that night, and Joe said he had a meeting with a donor to The Academy, Joan announced "I think I'll take the train home this evening. It's been a wonderful visit. I'm so glad I came. You've all inspired me, and I want to get to work on my next painting."

"My appointment's near Grand Central" Joe said, "We'll take a taxi. That way we'll have time for a glass of wine at the hotel next door."

Chapter Thirty-three

Joan decided that her mother would be her next subject. She felt a little ashamed at how she had eschewed an evening with Sarah, and wondered if her mother had sometimes avoided spending time with her.

Joan's mother was from an old Bostonian family. She'd come out as a debutant instead of going to college. She'd married a Harvard professor and settled in a house her parents gave her on Beacon Hill.

The marriage to Joan's father had been a mistake. Despite becoming a teacher at Harvard, he was a Liberation Catholic with radical ideals about pedagogy. Joan and her sister adored him. Their mother fought with him about everything, until he died before reaching the age of fifty.

Joan decided to paint her mother looking at herself in a mirror. As she started sketching she realized that this would be ridiculously difficult, but she felt that her mother was egging her on, telling her she would never be able to do her justice in a portrait.

Joan concentrated for a while on sketching her mother's clothes. She remembered them exactly: black high heels, silk stockings, a herringbone wool skirt, a cream colored silk blouse and a jacket that matched the skirt.

To her chagrin Joan realized she had no clear memory of her mother's face! None at all! She considered making up a face for her. Who would know? There was nobody living who remembered her. But that would be lying. And lying with paint seemed even worse than lying with words. Joan let the face go and made her mother's hands as exact as possible with the wide wedding ring. She placed pearls around her mother's neck, but there she was back at the face.

She began sketching her mother's mouth, open and angry, closed and peaceful, snarling with sarcasm. She tried many mouths, but ended up with a mouth that looked more sad than angry. Joan made her mother's cheekbones high, because she knew that's how her mother would want them. And then she came to her mother's eyes. She had no idea what color they were.

When her mother berated Joan for whatever reason, Joan fixed her eyes on the ground with a smirk on her mouth thinking what an idiot her mother was. Joan couldn't remember ever looking at her mother in her anger, wondering why she was so upset, or admitting that she herself had been foolish in what she had done. Joan remembered shouting at her mother but not looking at her as she shouted. She squinted as she sketched and erased until Joan made her mother's eyes filled with unshed tears. Suddenly, there they were! They were just as Joan remembered. It suddenly became clear that her mother had been desperately unhappy as well as angry!

"Oh, Mom!" Joan said aloud as her own eyes filled with tears. Joan put her pencils and eraser down and went to the kitchen area to pour herself a glass of wine. She took it to one of the chairs near the window and sat down facing Main Street which was now dark. As she sipped she cried. They weren't her tears; they were her mother's which were finally being allowed to flow.

Chapter Thirty-four

When Joan's father was alive December was a time of glorious church music. Her father took her and her sister Marianne to every concert being held in the Boston area, including the Messiah sing alongs. Joan was a teenager when her father died. For a long time her desire to go to church was overwhelmed by her anger at God for taking her father.

Alejandro loved music and went to all the concerts that took place in and around Hudson as Christmas approached. He too had been brought up singing Handel's Messiah more than once each December. Joan was dubious when he invited her to join him. She pictured not remembering anything, and standing silent and bereft in a crowd of singing strangers.

But that was not what happened. The alto line of the Messiah choruses came roaring back from her heart into her voice. At the same time someone singing the base line sounded so much like her father that it made her heart pound with joy.

She and Alejandro always spoke to each other in Spanish. It was Alejandro's first language. Joan had studied Spanish intensely when her husband was in the mountains of Nicaragua fighting the Contras. She had married him without their knowing each other's language, and she was determined to learn Spanish so they could talk together when he returned. But Oscar had been killed in the mountains, and Joan's fluency in Spanish was something she was eager to share.

As Christmas drew near, Alejandro told her, "My girls are going to Beth's mother, and my son is staying in California. What are your plans for Christmas?"

"Sarah and the family are going south to see the Miami City Ballet perform."

"And you?"

"They invited me to join them, but…" She shrugged rather than finishing her sentence.

"How about if you come to my house Christmas Eve and we have a fire in the hearth and cook tamales over it. Then we'll sing Christmas carols until we go to Midnight Mass."

"That sounds perfect."

On Christmas Eve they laughed a lot as Alejandro taught Joan how to make tamales. They lined the dried corn husks with masa dough and then filled their centers with cooked beef. They wrapped the corn husks tightly and steamed them. When the tamales were finally ready to eat, they enjoyed them with celebratory gusto. Soon after they set out for midnight Mass.

The church in Hudson was lit mostly by candles. It was full to overflowing with many people standing behind the pews shoulder to shoulder, and with children of all ages holding hands with siblings as they elbowed their way through the crowds to seek out their friends and cousins. Joan and Alejandro held hands as well. Joan felt that she had somehow found her way back to the first Christmas and the original barn, and that she was being kept warm not only by the crowds but also by the gentle breath of unseen cows and sheep.

When they left the church, snow was coming down in blinding waves. They held hands tightly as they carefully trod through the six inches or so already on the ground. They didn't talk about Alejandro driving Joan home that night. No words were needed. Instead they both entered the house to find it cold and dark. The power was off.

Alejandro quickly built up the fire in the hearth. He pulled the cushions and pillows off the couch and brought blankets from the beds and made a warm nest for them in front of the fire. Leaving their overcoats and hats and scarfs on, they settled in, sleeping back to back with blankets above and below them.

Christmas morning, the electricity was on but the house was still cold. Alejandro told Joan that he had signed up to help cook and serve breakfast at a Catholic Worker center a few blocks away. "Since the roads may not be plowed yet, perhaps you'd like to join me."

Joan felt that her father was encouraging her as she and Alejandro made their way down the street, with coffees-to-go in their hands. They joined about a dozen other volunteers making coffee and scrambling eggs with bacon and home fries. The line of hungry people was already stretching round the block. Joan started serving scrambled eggs from a large frying pan that was refilled every few minutes. When she noticed the clock on the wall, she realized she'd been there almost four hours, and she was having the best Christmas of her adult life.

Chapter Thirty-five

Seamus had trouble understanding what a Guatemalan farm worker was telling him. It made no sense. The family had driven to the bookstore after dark assuming Seamus would be working late, or perhaps planning to leave him a note.

The bookstore was closed and locked, but Seamus was working late, and when he heard a banging on the door he made his way down the steep stairs as quickly as possible and unlocked the door and peered out into the dark.

A farm worker stood there shivering. Seamus invited him into the store and turned on the electric light. Then he realized the man was someone he had an appointment with in the morning. Could the farmer be confused about the time?

"Can I help you?" Seamus asked in Spanish.

"My wife and I cannot meet tomorrow morning with the teachers. We are driving south now to get away from the cold."

"But the teacher is coming in specially on her vacation to talk about Reina with you. Reina has been missing a lot of school and she's not understanding ...."

"Reina is a good girl. She's been taking care of her little

brother while her mother cleans houses. We need a vacation."

Seamus was surprised by how angry he felt. The family had arrived in October, and it had been quite a push to get the three children settled into school as quickly as possible with the necessary vaccines. And then he'd found a job for the father at a plastics factory, which he remembered now, closed down for three months in the winter because of the cost of heating.

Seamus huffed and puffed inwardly at how little warning they'd given him and the teacher, and he wondered what would they have done if he hadn't been working late?

"Thank you for letting me know," he said, more or less deadpan. The farmer quickly shook Seamus's hand and ran back to the car, got in, and after a few tries got the motor running, and roared off. Seamus shivered as he stood there waving, realizing that the car was full of family. He thought how much he would love to drive south with Maggie, to let the sun warm them through.

He turned off the lights and locked the front door. Then he got into his van to drive toward Hudson to pick up clients who needed rides to the evening health clinic. As he drove, he realized he wasn't angry so much as envious.

He'd sometimes envied colleagues on the police force who made important arrests. He'd sometimes envied able-bodied men in general since his accident. But now he was envying his clients!

Seamus stood leaning against the wall of a small stuffy examining room interpreting for the farm worker who was lying on his stomach on the exam table describing the back pain that kept him awake each night after a long day of working in the fields. When the doctor offered to write a note prescribing rest for a week, the farm worker said no thank you because he couldn't afford to let go of a week's wages. Many of Seamus's clients worked long hours six or seven days a week to support their families in their home countries whom they often didn't see for years.

When the clinic closed for the night, and Seamus drove his clients back to their farms, he went to the pub on Warren Street and downed a few beers. It was crowded as he knew it would be. The conversations all around him and the loud music on the stereo helped him to concentrate on his question.

"How come the father of a migrant family from Guatemala feels free to go on vacation, and I don't? What will happen to his daughter because her parents have blown off their appointment with her worried teacher? How would these farm workers manage without me?"

Suddenly the noisiness all around him seemed to go silent, as he heard loud and clear inside his head. *They would do just fine.*

As a policeman walking the beat in East Boston, Seamus had quickly learned Spanish and made friends with the Latino families, especially with the parents of boys who had been coerced into being members of street gangs. He had sometimes managed to bring peace when a battle was brewing. He had gloried in these victories.

He had also loved his second career of welcoming migrant workers into his part of upstate New York. Finding schools and daycare for the children, and healthcare and food stamps for the parents made him feel a little larger than himself, made him feel glad to be alive.

But now? He felt grateful for the conversations, the laughter, the loud music that surrounded him as he asked himself what he was envying in this migrant family's difficult life? He turned the question over and over as though it were a ball of string that he couldn't find the end of.

He asked himself again, what would happen to these migrants if I weren't here to help them? To his chagrin the answer was loud and clear that they would find some other way to manage. Then he dared himself to ask what would happen to him if there was nobody who needed help?

Suddenly he needed air. He put money on the counter and fled for the door. Out on the sidewalk, he breathed the cold air deep into his lungs. He'd found the source of his envy. His clients were generous with each other, but they did not need to be helping someone in order to feel good about themselves.

Chapter Thirty-six

The next morning he met with Reina's righteously angry teacher in an almost empty school. He told her that Reina was missing classes because she was caring for a young sibling while her mother cleaned houses.

"That's against the law! Did you tell him that! Reina won't graduate from high school if she keeps missing classes! She's very intelligent but desperately ignorant. Don't they want to give her a chance to find a good job or even go to college?"

After the meeting he called Joan. "Can I take you out to lunch?"

"Do you mean today?"

"Yes, if you're free."

He arrived at the restaurant early, but Joan was already there. She'd chosen a table in the far corner near the wood burning stove. She stood up when she saw him. She was wearing a sky blue woolen sheath, which hung perfectly on her thin frame, and a necklace of many colored beads. Her white hair was cut very short. Her face was wrinkled in every direction, but her smile gave him the impression of a rising sun.

Seamus gave Joan a long hug before they sat down. His

niece and Joan's stepson were married, and living with their children in Joan's house in Nicaragua. He and Joan were family.

Joan was sipping a glass of white wine. When the waitress appeared Seamus ordered a Corona. As soon as she was gone, Joan asked, "You don't have bad news from Malpaisillo do you?"

"No, dear, no; I'm sorry if I worried you. I need your advice, perhaps even your help."

"Seamus, what's this about?"

At this moment the waitress returned with the Corona. Joan ordered a caesar salad with anchovies and Seamus asked for the hamburger special.

Once alone again, he took a minute or two with an inward sigh before he told her, "I'm thinking of giving up Bienvenido."

"What's happened?"

"In six years I'll be eighty. I want to do something different while I have the time."

"What do you want to do?"

"I want to go back onto the streets."

"Really?"

"No, not really. I mean of course really. That's what I want but that's not going to happen. I don't know what…"

"What about your clients?"

"Maybe they could come to you."

"To me?"

"You're a wonderfully welcoming person, and you speak Spanish. I can give you a list of where to take people for help."

Joan stared at him for a minute before saying, "Seamus, I'm almost eighty!"

"You have Latino friends, Joan. And some of them are here legally. Perhaps one of them could work with you and then take over when you were ready to retire."

Joan was silent for a long time.

Finally Seamus asked, "Do you want to think about it?"

"No, dear, I don't need to think about it. A year ago I would have loved to take it on. I might have even come north from Malpaisillo in order to take it on. But since I've come back, feeling useless and a little desperate, things have begun to change, I mean I have begun to change."

"In what way?"

"I'm painting, Seamus. I'm painting portraits."

"I didn't know you were a painter."

"While Oscar and his children were fighting the Contras in the mountains, I got to know Isaura. She was a painter from Managua. Her husband was in the mountains with Oscar.

"Isaura painted portraits of our neighbors' husbands, wives, and adult children who were fighting in the mountains. When the families did not have photographs, they would describe the person to Isaura. She was able to listen with her heart as well as her head, and little by little she would work on the portrait until the family said, 'Yes, that looks just like him!'

"Isaura lived with me and she gave me painting lessons."

Joan's face was lit up as though she'd been describing falling in love. "Here's to painting!" Seamus said as he gently clinked her wine glass with his beer bottle.

That evening Seamus visited his friends Urbelino and Magdalena. Years before he'd managed to bring Carlos, their young son, to the United States from Mexico by pretending to be Carlos's grandfather. Urbelino worked in the fields of a nearby farm, and Magdalena worked in the farm's office.

Seamus arrived at their trailer at supper time. He was immediately invited to join them. As Seamus ate Magdalena's delicious soup, he told them in Spanish, "I am thinking of retiring from Bienvenido."

"Are you well?" They both asked hurriedly.

"Yes, I'm healthy, but I am ready for something new. I've been thinking, Magdalena, that you would be the perfect new manager of Bienvenido. You are speaking more and more English. You are friendly and welcoming and you know how to use computers. I could show you all the other things you need to know."

Magdalena turned to Urbelino. They looked at each other in silence for a few minutes. Then Magdalena said, "I'd be helping people support their families back home. Can we afford to have me not work here?"

"Yes, my love, we can." Urbelino assured her. I know how

much you'd love to do this."

"We wouldn't be here without you, Seamus; I'd be continuing your important work."

"It would make me very happy if you would take this on. You would be the perfect person to do it because of who you are and your experiences. You would be an inspiration to people." Seamus held out his hand and Magdalena took it in hers.

Maggie was working late at the bookstore. Seamus stood for a minute in the open doorway and stared at her, loving her, and wondering what she would think of what he'd done.

She looked up with a frown as she felt the night air come in. And then she stared at him and began to smile. "You did it!" she said. "You climbed down from your prancing steed. You're no longer battling the windmills of School Boards and Labor Departments and Hospital Billing offices. You're just one of us now with your feet on the ground. And you're looking so happy I have to hug you."

As Seamus felt her body against his, and her gentle peck on both his cheeks, he knew he'd done the right thing.

As he drove home to Hudson, he asked himself how Maggie had known that it was time to let go of Bienvenido? Was she able to know what he was thinking before he even thought it? Did she know how much he thought about her, how much he longed for her?

Even if she knew, how could she respond to his longing if

he kept all signs of it hidden? Was it time to be honest with her? High time!

Chapter Thirty-seven

The next day Seamus presented Magdalena with his computer. "Won't you need it for other things?" she asked.

"I don't know yet what I'm going to be doing, but I'm positive it won't involve working with a computer."

Magdalena and Seamus spent two days in the office going through all the forms that people wanted help with filling out. Then he took her to the schools, the daycares, the clinics, the emergency room at the hospital and the police station, and introduced her as the new head of Bienvenido.

The next week he took her to the farms. He introduced her to the owners, and to the workers who had stayed on through the winter. At the end of that week he shook her hand formally in her new office and said, "It's all yours. Here's a key to the van, and a key to Treehouse Books in case you need to see people when the store is closed."

Magdalena had tears in her eyes. "Thank you, Seamus."

"You're welcome." Seamus turned away from her, and with Olaf at his heels, slowly descended the steep stairs from the office to the main floor of the store.

Maggie was at her desk surrounded by customers. Seamus put a log in the wood stove, and looked around. He had no idea what to do with himself. Finally he took his coat off the coat tree behind Maggie's desk and Olaf and he went out into the cold. Seamus walked carefully along the dirt road that had recently been plowed and was somewhat icy. He watched where he was stepping; he had the feeling of no longer existing. It was similar to how he'd felt when Rose died, and then again after the accident when his prosthetic foot meant he could no longer walk the streets as a policeman. As his body warmed up, he remembered that both of those times had felt like the end of his life. Well he was still here! What would come next?

First things first. He was hungry, and Maggie had looked tired. He decided to turn around, walk back to the store and begin his new life by driving into town and surprising Maggie by getting Chinese takeout for their supper.

Chapter Thirty-eight

Joan was rushing to get to the art supply store in Hudson before it closed. She pulled her apartment door shut, turned toward the stairs, missed the first step and fell down the entire steep stairway!

The pain made it almost impossible for her to breathe and she couldn't move her legs. She reached toward the doorknob of the street door but she was nowhere near touching it. She called for help but Carleton Books was closed, and her shouts were answered by the wind and rain banging against the door to the street. It wasn't locked, but the only reason anyone would open it would be to visit her, and the howling wind and drenching rain made that unlikely.

She heard her phone ringing in the apartment. She heard herself telling whoever it was that she would call them back.

As evening came on, the hallway became dusky and then dark and then pitch black. Her phone rang on and off and the wind and rain threw themselves against the door.

Until the door flew open and someone fell heavily onto her. His surprise and her pain made them both shout! As quickly as he could, he pulled himself off of her and stood up.

They couldn't see each other but she could feel how soggy he was as he dripped rain onto her.

"Are you okay?" he asked "I was just leaning against the door. I didn't mean to hurt you."

He opened the door to go back out into the storm when Joan shouted, "Please. I need help!" Under the street light she could see him looking unsure as to what to do, but then he turned around, closing the door behind him to keep the elements at bay.

Joan reached into her jacket pocket and was grateful to feel her keys. "Could you please go upstairs and use the phone to call 911 for me? I can't move my legs. Here are my keys."

He took a deep breath before he put his hand out for them, "Okay, lady if you're sure." Then he carefully climbed over her and pulled himself up the stairs holding on to the banister. It took him a few tries to unlock the door, and once he was in the apartment it took him a few minutes to find a light switch, but when he did the blessed light shone down on Joan and she felt hopeful again.

After a while he came back into the stairwell where he found the light switch that lit the hall. Joan stared up at him but could see very little. He seemed wrapped in rags held together with a sopping blanket. His gray hair and beard as well as the blanket were all still dripping. He called down, "They're coming. Do you want me to lock this door again?"

"Yes please," Joan said. "Thank you so much. You've saved my life."

"I think I'll be moving on," he said, as he handed her back the keys. Before she could get her hand into her other pocket to reach for her wallet, he'd climbed over her again and said, "Good luck, lady" as he slipped out the door into the rain and wind, and carefully closed it behind him.

Chapter Thirty-nine

Joan was taken to the hospital in Hudson. When the social worker asked whom they should call, Joan didn't know who to suggest.

She'd heard only once from Alejandro since Christmas morning. He'd called to tell her that his children's Christmas gift was a cruise along the coast of South America. "They want me far away so they can hire people to make changes on the house."

"Changes?"

"The changes that the realtor told them would make a big difference in the price I could get. I will miss you hugely and will call you as soon as I get back."

Spending Christmas with Alejandro had made her feel that she was beginning a new life, a life of laughter and joy, music and painting. She felt that all possibilities of life were ahead of her. But now she remembered he had not told her when he'd be back. Perhaps this talk of a cruise was his way of saying goodbye. Perhaps Christmas for him had been the realization that she was too old, and he wanted to be free.

With Alejandro gone, there really was no one that Joan cared about knowing where she was. Then she remembered that the angel, as she thought of him, had locked her door. Sage had a key to her apartment. The social worker called

Sage who appeared the next morning with a small suitcase of clothes, some mail, and a brand new copy of "Barchester Towers."

"Do you know Trollope? He's my favorite when I don't feel well. Your daughter called while I was in your apartment. I didn't answer the phone. She left a message sounding very annoyed that you hadn't picked up. Do you want me to call her?"

"No thank you, no, please don't." Joan said, feeling surprisingly urgent about it. "She already complains about my living at the top of a flight of stairs. She's convinced I'm going to have a heart attack as I climb them and she'll have to take care of me."

"Do you find the stairs so bad?"

"No, not at all, and the bannisters you put in make them completely comfortable. But, Sarah would like to turn back the clock so that she'd be young enough to dance again. My getting older is an annoying reminder of her own age."

"How are you doing?"

"I'm doing okay. I've got various fractures in my left leg, and my right hip needs to be replaced. But I'm going to be fine."

After Joan had been in the hospital for about a week, a social worker visited her to arrange the next phase of her recovery. "There's no way we can send you home with those steep stairs. It could be months before you'll be able to get up and down them. There's a place near here called The Highlands. It's mostly an old age home but it has a rehabilitation wing. I've already called them and they have a bed available. We need to move you somewhere by tomorrow because we've done all we can for you, and the hospital is filling up."

Joan longed to complain and laugh with Alejandro about the irony of her staying in the place they both disliked so much. But she still hadn't heard from him. She was trying to ready herself for the possibility that she never would hear from him again.

"Are there any other places?" She asked the social worker, who looked young enough to be playing hooky from high school.

"The truth is that's the best place within fifty miles. I wouldn't feel comfortable sending you anywhere else."

Chapter Forty

Joan was sent by ambulance and given a room with a window looking out on the parking lot. There was nothing, nothing at all, to complain about, but as soon as she was put into bed and tucked in too tightly, she felt as though she were in prison. Her stay in the hospital had been covered by insurance. The economics of staying at The Highlands was more complicated, but she was told they could deal with it once she was settled in.

Mary, the physical therapist, came three times a week and took Joan to the physical therapy room on the same floor. Mary hauled her out of the wheelchair and stood her up between two bars that were hip height and held on to a strap around her waist while Joan walked forward and backward. "You really need to do this every day. You'll heal faster that way. It's not good being in the wheelchair so much. I've spoken to the nurses and they've said they'll try to fit it into their schedules, but everyone is busy."

One morning Joan asked the lady who cleaned her room to place two chairs back to back with some space in-between. After the cleaning lady left, Joan managed to pull herself out of the wheelchair to stand for a few moments between the chairs. But when she tried to walk, one of the chairs slipped and she landed in an extremely painful heap on the floor.

After that there was no more talk of nurses helping her to walk. One nurse warned her that if she did something like that again she might be tied into the wheelchair. Sometimes as Joan lay on her back in the bed, she pushed the bedclothes out of the way, and lifted her legs into the air as high as possible and pretended to walk on the ceiling.

"What in Hell are you doing!" Joan's legs were grabbed with heavy force and pushed down against the bed.

"Get off me, God damn it!" Joan shouted before seeing who it was who had attacked her.

"Mom!" Sarah spurted with horror. "Your naked legs were in the air and your nightgown round your hips. Are you insane? Is that why you're here?"

While her daughter shouted at her, Joan struggled to sit up. Finally she succeeded and was able to lean forward and drag the bedclothes up to her waist.

"How could you not call me? I had to hear about you from a social worker. Can you imagine how that made me feel?"

"Sarah," Joan said, puffing a bit from her exertion as well as the anger she tried to hide, and the pain that Sarah's rough manipulations had caused on her legs, "I didn't call you because I'm fine. I'll be back on my feet very soon and back in my apartment. I didn't call you because there's nothing to worry about. And I know how busy you are."

"Indeed I am. I gave up three classes, and two auditions, in order to come here." Then in a softer voice she confided,

"Mom, the nurse said you're not cooperating! She said I had to come to make sure you don't get hurt."

Joan was speechless with anger.

"She said you could fall again at any time, and next time you might take a nurse or another patient down with you!"

"Nobody was hurt. I was just trying to do the exercise I'd been told that I needed! To her horror Joan realized that a sob was coming. She stopped speaking and breathed deeply three times until she was able to ask, "How are the kids?"

"The kids are fine, Mom. We're all fine now that we know you are safe here and being well taken care of."

"Safe?"

"You're not going to fall down those stairs again; you're not going to set fire to your apartment by forgetting something on the stove; you're not going to get mugged because you're out by yourself in the evening. You're safe!"

The horror that her daughter's words were creating made Joan not able to speak for a minute. Perhaps this was good, because she had time to put her words into full sentences when she finally said, "Sarah, I was in a rush and I tripped. I've never set fire to anything. And muggings don't happen in Carleton. I've always been safe!"

"Mom, listen to me. I'm speaking for the kids as well as for Joe, who would be here too except he's in Italy with the senior choir. Wouldn't it be a good idea to stay here? It would make it so much easier for us because we could stop worrying about you. I've been looking into the possibility. You can keep this room where you can watch people coming and going.

Joan felt as though she'd fallen down a flight of stairs, set her apartment on fire, and been mugged all in one swift blow. She couldn't breathe at first and then began to cough and cough as though her lungs were determined to eject what her ears were hearing.

"Listen, Mom, I'm sure you'll like it in the long run," Sarah continued. "I've already told the director that you like to paint. She said that although you couldn't use oil paint because of the smell, and that watercolors would be too messy, you could always make wonderful drawings with colored pencils. You'll make friends here, Mom, friends who speak English, friends you can play Scrabble with, friends who are living in this country legally! You'll like it. I know you will. And you'll enjoy knowing how happy we are in the city because you're here, rather than risking life and limb out on your own."

After a very long silence, Sarah continued, "Listen Mom I've got to go. I have a train to catch. Don't worry about anything. I love you."

Joan didn't actually hear the last word because Sarah said it as she strode out of the room.

Joan's fury gave her the energy to throw the blankets back once more and reach toward the ceiling with her legs. But this time her legs could hardly move. It was as though gravity itself was pulling them down with extra force. Joan covered herself up again and lay still, as her breath began to find its own pace again. This was death, no this was worse than death. Joan had prided herself on being a good mother, at least to Sarah, and a good grandmother. Slowly as her fury ebbed into desperate sadness, she realized that maybe Sarah was right. Maybe Joan was harming her family by living independently? Maybe worrying about her was causing them to have less energy for their own lives. It certainly seemed to be true of Sarah. Maybe if she just lay still, let go of all thoughts of walking ever again, all would be well for those she loved.

Chapter Forty-one

Dear Seamus Carroll,

This is to share with you our great joy in having raised enough pledges of funds to purchase your house. We will call it "St. Rose's Refuge."

We are truly grateful to you for making the price below the market value, and we are grateful to our parishioners for raising the necessary funds.

We hope that you will be able to come to our ribbon cutting ceremony.

Best wishes from all of us, and God bless you in your generosity,

Father Gerald Brennan

The official letter was accompanied by a hand-written note,

Seamus,

Heartfelt thanks my friend – you're helping a great many women and children.

God bless, Gerald

The letter arrived the morning of Maggie's birthday. Seamus knew what day that was because Michael had asked for his advice about what sort of present she might like. He'd also asked, "Do you think you could have dinner with us? You know, to make it more like a celebration?"

"Of course, if you don't think she'd mind," Seamus agreed. "She may want to be quietly with you."

"We're quiet every evening. We need to make some noise. She's going to be seventy-two!"

"There's a new Japanese restaurant in Hudson. Do you think she'd like that?"

"That's awesome. We tried to make sushi a few nights ago without much success."

"Good, then that's our plan."

Seamus had no idea what present to get Maggie. Since hearing Rose tell him that he should marry her, he'd begun to let himself stare at Maggie when she was looking away. He didn't want to frighten her. He had no reason to think that she liked him. But he'd finally admitted to himself that he was a goner.

He didn't dare buy her a ring. Instead he found a turquoise necklace that he knew would look beautiful against her skin.

When he arrived at Treehouse Books on her birthday morning, Maggie was already at work. He gave her the dozen yellow roses he'd bought on the way,

"Oh, Seamus, roses in March — what a wonderful miracle."

"You, dear, have been my miracle." To Seamus's horror he felt himself blush.

Maggie filled the silence with, "They're absolutely beautiful. Thank you." Then as Seamus was still waiting for his blood to subside she continued, "Michael says we're going to meet you for supper this evening."

"Yes, good. I look forward to it," he said as he turned around and quickly left the bookstore just as Magdalena was coming in.

Seamus had forgotten about chopsticks. He'd often shared Chinese takeout with Caitlin and Malika. The girls had tried, with gales of laughter, to teach him how to eat with chopsticks. He hadn't cared how much they laughed at him, but with Maggie it was different. He didn't want Maggie to see that he was all thumbs as well as having only one foot. After carefully weighing the problem he decided it would be worse than cowardly to ask the waitress for a fork, so he desisted and prayed for help as he lifted the chopsticks and tried to remember finger by finger what his hand should be doing. Miracle of miracles, his hand seemed to remember. Maggie ordered sushi rolls for the table and it turned out they were very easy to get from the plate to the mouth. Maggie also ordered sake. Michael asked for ginger ale, and when it was Seamus's turn, remembering that Michael would be driving

Maggie home, he also asked for sake having no idea what it was. It proved to be tasty, smooth, and heartening all at the same time.

Warmed by the sake, Seamus took Gerald's letter out of his pocket to show to Maggie and Michael. "That's wonderful," Maggie said. "Now Rose will be remembered always as making that refuge possible."

Seamus sighed with pleasure as she said that. It had become clear to him that falling in love with Maggie was not changing his love for Rose. He stared at Michael and Maggie across the table. Maggie was sipping sake, but Michael was looking right at him. Seamus loved them both, right down to the toes on his good foot.

Michael decided it was time for presents. He pulled out of his pocket a small package. It turned out to be a statue of a black bear about three inches tall made out of a stone that had been smoothed until it felt like velvet. "It's a totem," Michael told them. "The Native Americans use them. This one represents and gives you —" and then he pulled out from his pocket a small card and read "healing power, courage and perseverance."

"Those are just the qualities I need more of." Maggie said with tears in her eyes. "Thank you so much, Michael!"

Seamus pulled from his pocket the box containing the necklace. "But you've already given me roses," Maggie said.

"See what you think of this," Seamus mumbled. "It may not be your kind of thing at all."

Maggie opened the box. Seamus was aggrieved that he hadn't thought of wrapping paper or even a ribbon. "Oh, Seamus, it's lovely! I love turquoise! Here, Michael, could you attach it for me?" After Michael carefully closed the clasp at the back of her neck, Maggie turned to face Seamus who found her beautiful beyond compare with the necklace shining against her bare skin.

From then on the evening seemed to have a glow to it. Maggie told stories about finding rare books in people's estate sales. Michael read aloud a letter from Father Paul about how much he missed Bash Bish Falls. Seamus told about meeting the snake on his birthday. There was a lot of laughter, and when they parted outside the restaurant under a sky lit brightly by stars, there were hugs and plans for future parties. Seamus headed down hill towards his apartment near the river feeling as though he was able to hold his head almost as high as the stars, while his feet, both real and hard plastic, seemed to be dancing on the sidewalk.

Chapter Forty-two

Joan was allowed to close her bedroom door only during the hour after lunch. The rest of the day, except for the three hours a week when the physical therapist taught Joan exercises she wasn't allowed to practice on her own, Joan sat in her nemesis, the wheelchair. Sarah had acquiesced to Highland's request that they tie Joan into this chair, "just to keep you safe, Mom."

Instead of feeling safe, Joan felt dead. She still had a body but she no longer tried to move any of it. She sat inert in the hallway where she was placed, "so you can enjoy seeing everyone, dearie" and waited for her body to die the way her heart and her imagination had.

Her grandchildren sent cards promising to visit. Joe was in Europe recruiting faculty for The Academy. Maggie wrote Joan a note, "Seamus and I were going to visit you last week but your daughter came to the store to say that it would be better if we waited for you to be more settled. She said we would make things worse for you by visiting now. So I'm making a pile of books to give you when it's the right time."

Sage had also sent a note, "I'm in San Francisco making West Coast paintings!"

Joan wondered what Alejandro would think of her when

he knew. He would say she'd been a cougar. He would say that she had pretended to be young, to be independent, to be able to go places and enjoy concerts. And that the results of her pretending had been falling down the stairs and never being able to walk again.

But during the hour after lunch when Joan was allowed to have her door shut, there was such a feeling of release when they untied her from the wheelchair and laid her back on her bed, that despite the risk of being caught, Joan got out of bed and practiced walking in place, back and forth between two chairs. She had learned to lean one chair against the wall and another against the bed and also to take off her socks so she wouldn't slip. She practiced walking forward and backward just the length of her arms so she wouldn't have to move the chairs while she walked. She also practiced lifting her knees as high as possible one at a time and then bending them backwards.

One afternoon, despite being very careful, she fell. It was the elderly man, who mopped the floors, who heard the thump and her curse. He opened her door and then quickly closed it again so he wouldn't be seen helping her get up off the floor.

"Please," Joan said, "don't tell anyone."

"Not on your life," he said, giving her a wink as he quickly slipped out of her room.

Chapter Forty-three

Suddenly the world thawed. The sun was brilliant in the blue sky without a cloud.

It was Seamus's birthday. He decided to celebrate by climbing Mt. Alander. He considered asking Michael if he wanted to join him, but Seamus thought that if the trail was too steep, he wanted to be by himself if he had to turn back.

The parking lot at the trailhead was empty. He headed down the path, loudly singing songs that he'd learned from the Texas Tornados' record, left by someone, along with a pile of books, in front of Maggie's door. He felt companioned by his own voice and by the humor and the love-sick lyrics.

The path started on a gentle slope downhill from the parking lot and across a field to a stream. After crossing the stream the path began its gentle climb. It was well worn, and Seamus was comfortable and confident of his footing for quite a while.

When the path became steep, Seamus bent over and pulled himself up with his hands grabbing boulders and branches, and digging his feet as deep into the earth as they would go.

It was at this point that he heard a noise that he did not recognize. It was a hiss. He looked ahead on the path and saw a snake, with an intricate design all over its long body, curled round and round with its face facing Seamus's face and its tiny ears alert.

Seamus very slowly unfolded his body until he was standing on his legs. His balance was precarious. He dared not step backward for fear that he would slip and fall face down onto the snake. He stood as still as possible, trying to make it clear to the snake that he was benign.

He knew that he wasn't benign as a species. The snake made it clear to him, almost as though it were shouting, that people were callously destroying the natural world.

They stared at each other in silence.

Finally, the snake uncoiled itself and slipped into the bushes.

Seamus took a deep breath, reached his hands back down to the ground and began backing downhill, clinging to the boulders the way he'd come up.

Later that afternoon Caitlin called her father, "Can I take you out for supper at the pub to celebrate how ancient you are?"

"That sounds fine with me. What about Malika?"

"She has auditions…. Actually I want to talk with you about something, just the two of us."

"Is everything okay with you and Malika?" Was the first thing Seamus said as he stood up, when Caitlin arrived at the table he had chosen. He remembered how horrified he'd been years before when Caitlin had told him about her love for Malika, but now Malika felt like a second daughter.

"No, Dad, nothing like that. Not to worry."

"Oh good!" He kissed her cheek and sat down with a sigh.

Caitlin's smile beamed at him. Perhaps she was remembering his old feelings as well, he wondered. In any case his daughter looked radiant.

They ordered burgers and beer.

"How does it feel to be so old?"

"I climbed a mountain this morning; I didn't get to the top but I got pretty high."

He then told her about it, and she asked, "Were you frightened?"

"Yes, somewhat. I did note that there was no one to help if I got bitten."

"Oh, Dad!"

"But I didn't get bitten. Tell me your news."

"We're going to have a baby."

"How?" As soon as he heard what he had said, he blushed with the foolishness of it.

"I'm already pregnant, Dad."

"My goodness." This time he told himself, *Don't ask any more questions! Better not to know.*

"That's wonderful, my love." He said gazing into his daughter's eyes.

Chapter Forty-four

As Spring began to change the world, Seamus felt as though he was stuck in neutral and couldn't get back into gear. Without a job, a reason to get out of bed, he often didn't, until a headache told him that he needed coffee. He wandered aimlessly around Hudson pretending interest in antique shops and art galleries. The one place he wanted to be was at Treehouse Books, more specifically in his office.

He had to get out of town. Once he'd made the decision, the wheels began to turn and he got a phone call from Gerald. "We are celebrating the purchase of your house..."

"My former house"

"Your former house, with a one night production of Say Goodnight, Gracie. It's a one-man play about George Burns's life. My old friend, Nicholas McMann, from the Abbey Theater in Dublin, is going to perform it. This is a celebration and a fund raiser. If you would consider coming here and being praised for your generosity, it would add a great deal to the project. Nicholas will be staying here at the rectory. There's more than enough room for you as well. I think you would enjoy each other. Please say you'll come."

Nicholas McMann, grey haired and slightly stooped,

performed the story of George Burns from his impoverished youth to his and Gracie's celebrity. People of all ages in the large audience laughed and cried and laughed again. By the end of the play Seamus felt he'd been on a long journey with George Burns filled with the joys of a loving marriage and a love of acting.

After the production, Nicholas and Seamus returned with Gerald to the rectory. There was a fire in the hearth which cast lights and shadows on the three of them. Seamus stared with surprise at Nicholas, who now looked old and a little frail, nothing at all like the George Burns character he had been on stage.

Seamus leaned back in the upholstered chair, and let its comfort surround him. Gerald and Nicholas shared memories of their childhoods in Ireland. Seamus thought of his childhood, growing up in the North End of Boston. As a teenager he had done a fair amount of fighting against the kids who told him to go home to Ireland. He fought to prove that he was home no matter what they thought of him. He thought of George Burns beginning his career as a singer at age seven and exploring life in all its ups and downs until he was one hundred.

It was almost as though remembering the play sent fresh air into the room and into Seamus's heart. Also, these men, whose conversation he was enjoying, were very alive and active, and they were more or less his age. Burns had acted into his 90s. What had made Seamus get so stuck? He didn't know, but asking the question gave him a feeling of energy, of new possibilities.

He listened more intently to the conversation of these friendly men, one of whom he'd known for many years. He felt relaxed with them in a new way; he was one of them, with many past experiences over a long life and a future open wide to surprises.

Chapter Forty-five

Seamus left for home early the next morning, but instead of returning to his apartment in Hudson, he drove straight to Treehouse Books. It was Wednesday, the day the store was open only in the mornings, the day of the week when Maggie was free to explore estate sales in the afternoons. As he drove, about ten miles over the speed limit, across Massachusetts, Seamus repeated to himself again and again, "I hope she has nothing planned!" As soon as he arrived at Treehouse Books, just before closing time, he swung open the door to the store and announced, to the dawdling customers as well as to Maggie, "Will you come with me to The Globe, to see The Importance of Being Earnest? Caitlin says it'll be a hit."

Ignoring her customers, and surprising Seamus, Maggie went up to him without a word, and kissed him on the cheek, before answering, looking into his eyes, "I'd love to. How wonderful to have you back."

This was the opening performance of The Importance of Being Earnest, and in order to enhance the celebration, The Globe had arranged to have the Café on Main Street make two hundred cucumber sandwiches which the theater sold with cups of tea before the matinee. The people who didn't know the plot of the play thought this was odd but nice, but the people who knew the play laughed in delight at the idea, and Caitlin got many compliments.

Caitlin gave Seamus and Maggie front row seats. "It's nice to see you guys looking so happy," she said as she kissed her dad's cheek and hurried backstage.

As they watched the play, Maggie laughed happily every few minutes. Seamus had no idea why she was laughing but he enjoyed the sound of her laughter immensely. For him the play was unintelligible. The words were in English but the sentences made no sense.

When he gave up trying to understand what was happening, and let the dialogue just be noise, he began to look more carefully around the stage.

The program said that the place was London and its suburbs, and the time was the late 1800s. Seamus didn't know what a London apartment would look like in the late 1800s, but the stage right in front of him made him feel that he was sitting in a rich gentleman's claustrophobic city apartment with depressing gray and brown striped wallpaper, and out-sized, over lacquered heavy furniture, a gray Persian rug, and a quietly ticking Grandfather clock. There were uncomfortable-looking chairs and little tables covered with cups and saucers that looked as though they were about to fall. The room looked uncomfortable, ugly, and awkward, but it looked real!

The next morning Seamus drove back to The Globe to talk to the man who had designed the set. Ron looked to be in his sixties. His hair was thick and gray and needed a cut. His beard was almost white. He wore painter's overalls over a tee shirt and was drawing on a large board when Seamus poked his face into the shed behind the theater. "Can I take you out to lunch?" Seamus asked.

"You talking about a roast beef sandwich at the pub?"

"That's what I'm talking about, with a couple of beers."

"How's right now?"

"Right now is just right."

Seamus drove them to the pub in Carleton and they settled in.

As soon as they'd ordered, Seamus said, "I don't know anything about gentlemen's houses in London, in the old days, but the set you made for Earnest seemed exactly right. How did you know what to do?"

"Malika and I look at books and magazines, whatever we can get our hands on, and then we talk. Based on that, I draw a possible set, and she usually agrees to it. I used to be an architect so the drawing part is easy."

"What made you go from architecture to set design?"

"My wife was acting at the Guthrie in Minneapolis; their set designer left in a huff about something, so I filled in for the emergency, and then… then I just stayed on.

"And now?"

"My wife ran off with one of the actors; I needed distance,

so here I am.

"Do you build the sets as well?"

"Yes, my dad was a carpenter and I helped him through college."

"Could you teach me how to be helpful to you?"

"Have you built stuff before?"

"I built a treehouse for my daughter and her friends when they were young. It didn't look like much but it withstood two hurricanes."

"That sounds like a good building. Our next play, Watch on the Rhine, involves a staircase. Would you like to work on that?"

"I'd like that a lot."

Back at the shed, Ron showed Seamus how to interpret his drawing for the staircase and then together they figured out how much lumber they would need. Ron gave Seamus the keys to The Globe's truck and Seamus drove to the hardware store to pick up the lumber.

The next day, Seamus sawed lengths of wood for each stair. The experience of sawing reminded him that he hadn't used the strength of his arms for a long time. He remembered the summer that he'd made the treehouse for Caitlin. Two neighbors had helped out, fathers of Caitlin's friends. None of them had had experience in building, but Seamus had bought a blueprint and they were determined to make it work and be safe. It was quite high up the tree but it had a railing all around it so that nobody would fall out by accident. When it was completed, all three fathers climbed into it and stomped around as roughly as possible showing themselves and the mothers of the five little girls how secure it was. The experience of building it together and watching it survive the storms had made the men good friends, which lasted until the girls went to different colleges and the families moved away. Seamus remembered his regret that they couldn't take the treehouse with them when he bought the house near the Catholic school where Rose was teaching. He had hoped it would be enjoyed by his grandchildren.

While Seamus sawed and sanded the steps, Ron worked on the frame for the stairs. Then he showed Seamus how to make the banisters. When everything came together, all the pieces fitting into each other and being carefully nailed in place, Ron and Seamus tramped up and down the stairs a couple of times and declared it finished and ready to be painted.

Seamus began to spend a lot of time at the shed. Ron had been working on his own for two months. "You've come just at the right time," he told Seamus. "My last assistant decided to design websites after he hit his thumb with a hammer for the third time."

Seamus tried to paint landscapes on backdrops, but his

landscapes looked like abstracts. Ron could paint mountains and shop windows and insides of living rooms, and everything else.

So Seamus stuck to carpentry. Ron taught him new things every day. Seamus took notes in a little notebook as he had done as a policeman. They didn't talk much as they worked except about the projects. But after work the two of them often sat together on a bench outside the shed drinking beer and watching the sun sink behind the hills.

On Monday nights, when The Globe was dark. Caitlin invited Ron and Seamus for supper and a business meeting. Malika told them about the plays that had been sent to the theater by hopeful playwrights and Caitlin described some of her old favorites that she was considering producing. They talked about what the audiences might like and about possible set designs for the plays they thought they'd do. After a few months of Seamus volunteering, Caitlin insisted on paying him a salary. "Ron says you're a real help. I don't want you to feel different because you're my dad."

"I don't," he told her. "I feel part of the team. It's not like being part of the police force, but there is a feeling that what I do helps things go forward."

"Everything you do, Dad, helps in myriad ways."

"I have no idea what you're talking about, but thank you."

Chapter Forty-six

Seamus wanted to talk with Father Paul. He wanted to tell him how grateful he was for his advice about talking with Rose. And, he had another quandary to ask Father Paul about.

Father Paul gave him exact directions about how to get from the train station at 125th street to the brownstone where he now lived. When Seamus knocked on the door of the apartment, Father Paul's brother, Tom, let him in and introduced himself. The narrow hallway was lined with framed family photos. Tom pointed out pictures of Father Paul and himself as young boys, and then in high school, and finally at Father Paul's ordination. There were also pictures of Tom and Janie's wedding, and of their children and grandchildren, and a picture of Janie graduating from nursing school.

Father Paul waited at the end of the hall as Tom explained each photograph. Once they got close enough, Seamus shook Father Paul's hand, and said, "Thank you, Father, for being willing to see me." He wanted to make it sound formal enough for Tom to get the idea that he wanted to be alone with the priest.

"You're most welcome," Father Paul said. "I think you told me that this is your first visit to New York City."

"Yes, it is. I've been to Yankee Stadium once to see a Red Sox game but we drove down and didn't go into the city."

"Well I was thinking that I would like to show you St. Patrick's Cathedral. What do you think?"

Seamus was about to say, "No need for that, all I really want is to talk with you," but he realized in time that Father Paul was giving them a reason to get out of the apartment, away from Tom. So he said, "I'd like that a lot."

"Don't forget your scarf," Tom said as Father Paul put on his grey wool coat.

"I won't; thank you," Father Paul told him. Tom and Seamus shook hands, and Father Paul led Seamus to the stairwell. They descended the stairs slowly, Father Paul being considerate of Seamus's prosthetic foot. As the door to the apartment building closed behind them, they breathed the cool air deep into their lungs. They walked back the way Seamus had come, south to 125th street and then east on the wide busy street past the Apollo Theater. Father Paul told him about the jazz he'd heard there. Then on to the Lexington Avenue subway station. "This will get us there in a jiffy," Father Paul said. They were talking in Spanish.

The subway left them off under Grand Central Station and they climbed up the stairs and out into the air. They walked west to Fifth Avenue which was wide and spacious. There they turned north. As they walked, Seamus glanced at the huge store-front windows to his right, with mannequins dressed in surprising fashions interacting with each other in front of backdrops of large photographs of the Eiffel Tower, a jungle waterfall, and the Statue of Liberty.

"Is the light green? Let's cross here," Father Paul said. He took Seamus's arm and led him across Fifth Avenue. Father Paul did not let go of Seamus's arm as he guided him down a wide path, with planters down the center of it, to a balcony overlooking an ice skating rink. It was presided over, or rather blessed by, a much-larger-than-life gilded bronze statue of Prometheus bringing fire to the world. The warming spring sun glinted off the golden statue as though spring itself was being nurtured by the flame.

Then Father Paul led Seamus back up the wide path to Fifth Avenue and they went a few steps further north so that Seamus could see the bronze statue of Atlas high on a pedestal holding the world on his shoulders with outstretched arms. The world was made of interweaving bronze circles through which Seamus could see the tops of skyscrapers and the sky itself.

As Seamus stared, Father Paul told him the Greek legend that Zeus had condemned Atlas to never be able to lay his burden down throughout eternity. After a few minutes Father Paul reached for Seamus's shoulder and said, "And now for Christianity." He turned Seamus to face Fifth Avenue traffic, and across from where they stood was St. Patrick's Cathedral.

Inside the Cathedral, the extraordinary spaciousness of the center aisle that seemed to Seamus to go on forever, was made intimate and welcoming by the niches along the lengths of the side walls. Each niche held a statue or painting of a saint or holy person as well as places for people to kneel in prayer before them. People could visit and pray with the saint of their choice in his or her niche, almost as though one were dropping in on them, in their own house, for a cup of tea and a conversation.

"Follow me," Father Paul said, speaking in Spanish. "I'm going to show you my favorite. I used to come here often." He walked quickly, lightly tapping with his white cane which created a river of emptiness as people drew back. Seamus followed close in his wake. They went toward the altar in the front and then bore right. They were in front of the painting of the Virgin of Guadalupe.

Father Paul sat down in a pew facing the image and Seamus sat down next to him. "My suggestion," Father Paul said softly, "is that we don't say anything for a while, that we simply let the image of the Virgin speak to us, and then we can talk later."

Seamus didn't ask blind Father Paul how on earth he was going to let the image of the Virgin speak to him. Instead he just sat back in the pew and stared.

After a while the image seemed to stare back. It's not that she lifted her head to look at him, but as he stared at her, he felt that she knew he was there. She seemed to know a great deal about him, perhaps everything, and most of all, she knew that in the end all would be well. Seamus closed his eyes and sat in her presence and her knowledge. He no longer wondered how Father Paul was doing the same. It was as though a light of healing and mercy and peace was surrounding them and all the other people who sat with them.

After a while Seamus felt a gentle warmth throughout his body, and then he felt Father Paul's hand covering his own. "Are you well?" Father Paul asked in Spanish. He used the familiar word for 'you' and Seamus answered him in the same way. They had become friends.

They left the Cathedral, and once again Paul said, "Follow me," and tapping lightly with his cane led Seamus eastward to Madison Avenue and then south to a coffee shop in the middle of the block. The man behind the counter called out, "Hello Father, Welcome."

"Thank you very much," Paul said, as he made his way into an area in the back where tall booths would give their conversation privacy.

When orders of coffee and hamburgers were brought to their booth, they settled back and sipped. Seamus stared at Paul. Paul's face was thin with lots of wrinkles but mostly those near his eyes seemed to come from smiling. His eyes themselves were clouded as though he were looking inwards. He smiled at Seamus now. "So, how are things going for you, Seamus?"

Seamus told Paul about his visit to Rose's grave. "I can't

thank you enough for suggesting I talk with her."

"I had the feeling when you called, that there was something new you wanted to talk about." Paul said.

"Yes, you're right." After a moment of leaning back against the booth, Seamus said, "I don't know if I've told you that my daughter, Caitlin, is in love with another woman." Seamus watched Paul closely but saw no signs of judgment on his face. "I was horrified at first," Seamus continued, "But after a lot of foolishness on my part, we created a ceremony to celebrate their becoming life partners."

Paul nodded but didn't speak.

"Now Caitlin has told me they are having a child, I assumed they were adopting, but Caitlin is actually pregnant with a stranger's sperm." To his chagrin Seamus realized that his voice sounded like a whine.

Perhaps because of the whine, Paul smiled broadly before he said, "She's always one step ahead of you, isn't she."

"Yes, I suppose that's a good way to put it," Seamus said glumly. "To me it seems that since I lost my foot, I can't keep up with her."

"Seamus, you lost your foot helping a stranger. Isn't that what we want to do as often as possible? Your lack of a foot has set you ahead not behind the rest of us. I didn't know you before, but I know you with only one foot to be generous and open hearted, wanting to follow God's will in every way possible. What more could you ask of yourself?"

Seamus didn't know what to say. Then Paul continued,

but switched to English. "Caitlin is pregnant. At this point the Church does not care how it happened. All there is to do is love the baby." Paul lifted up his coffee cup and waited for a moment until Seamus lifted his as well. They knocked them gently together as Paul said, smiling broadly, "Congratulations!"

Chapter Forty-seven

"Where'd you go with that limping guy?" Tom asked Paul as soon as he got back to the apartment.

"We went to St. Patrick's Cathedral."

"So, he's a Catholic? Was he born with that limp? I didn't like the look in his eye?"

"What do you mean?"

"I bet he's Irish. He just had the look of peering down his nose at us."

"Well I can't see his look but he doesn't talk that way. He used to be a policeman. His foot was mangled when he was helping someone who'd gotten stuck on the road at night. My guess is that after a few beers you and he would enjoy each other."

"But you two can get on without the beers?"

"Well as you said, he's a Catholic, I'm a priest. We're made for each other."

"Well maybe you want to get out of your collar and help me make supper?"

"I'd enjoy that," Paul said, which was close to the truth.

It was in the kitchen that Tom was most his old self. In the kitchen Tom told Paul what to do: peel the potatoes; wash the pots; set the table. Paul was his underling, his kid brother, grateful for his praise, but often made to feel a little inadequate about what he'd accomplished. They never mentioned the accident, but Paul felt that he was being watched extremely carefully so that no new accident could possibly happen, especially in the home kitchen.

Once supper was made and the table laid, they put the casserole in the oven to stay warm until Janie got home from the hospital. Tom watched television, and although he urged Paul to watch with him promising that he would tell him what was happening, Paul preferred playing the electric keyboard that Tom's son had left behind when he moved away. It was equipped with ear phones so Paul could play in the living room, keeping Tom company without disturbing him.

Chapter Forty-eight

It was the first week in May before Joan heard from Alejandro. "I was desperate! I called all the hospitals and the police. Finally I thought of Sage, thank God! I got back last week. I'm living in my granddaughter's basement apartment in New Jersey, while the realtor tries to sell my house. My kids are insisting I get a high price for it, too high so far for everyone who's looked at it. Anyway I'm coming to see you tomorrow. I'll leave here around dawn and get there as early as possible. I want to spend as much of the day there as possible."

That evening Joan talked with Alejandro in her head for hours. She told him that it would mean a great deal to her daughter and grandchildren if she stayed at the Highlands, out of the way, doing what she was told and not endangering anyone by attempting to live alone again. She told him again and again how old she was and that she had had a good life, with no regrets and that he who was still young should enjoy himself in the world and that she would enjoy receiving postcards from wherever he traveled.

Alejandro arrived around midmorning. The nurse hadn't yet tied Joan to the chair, and without thinking about it, Joan stood up from the wheelchair to give him a bear hug. When she let go of him, she flopped back down surprised that she'd been so upright.

"Let's get out of here!" Alejandro said a little breathlessly. Without saying a word to anyone in charge he quickly pushed the wheelchair to the front door, and then pressed a button on the wall, and they were out in the fresh air.

Joan hadn't been outside the building since she'd arrived. Bright yellow daffodils seemed to nod a welcome to her from across the patio. Near the sunny daffodils were gloriously red and dark purple tulips making her gasp at their beauty.

"Do you want to try to walk holding on to the wheelchair?" Alejandro asked.

"I don't see the point of it." Joan said glumly. "Sarah is insisting that I stay on here so I don't worry the family."

"Stay on here!"

"Yes, she says that my being on my own has been making things difficult for the family because they never know when I will fall down the stairs or set the building on fire. So for their sake I should stay here where there are no stairs and I'm not allowed near a stove."

"She sounds like the granddaughter I'm living with who keeps checking my closet for hidden liquor. It's been fifteen years, but she still doesn't trust me. Juana dear, let's take a stroll for my sake if not for your own."

Joan loved hearing Alejandro call her Juana; it included her life in Nicaragua as well as here; it made her feel whole. She answered him in Spanish, "Not here. I'm not sure I'm even allowed to. Let's go somewhere where we won't be seen by anyone. The Physical Therapist says I'm ready to walk. But she's only here three days a week, and the staff doesn't listen to her when she's not around."

Alejandro wheeled her along a path that led toward the back of the main building. Then he put on the brakes of the wheelchair and said in Spanish, "Let's walk here. The view is beautiful and you can see it better when you're standing up." He reached for both her hands and gently pulled her to her feet. He tucked one of her arms under his elbow and they began to slowly stroll. Joan had no fear of falling. Alejandro held her tight against his side. When she stumbled slightly his arm brought her upright again instantly. After a few minutes Joan stopped worrying about her legs and simply walked, staring with joy at the valley below them, and at the spaciousness of the world.

They strolled along the winding paths to where he had parked his car. "Let's go out for lunch," he suggested.

"I don't think I'm allowed to." Joan said doubtfully, "and I don't have my purse."

"I'm inviting you, Juana. You don't need a purse. Have you signed anything saying you'll stay here?"

"Nobody has asked me to sign anything. I think they assume I'm too feeble."

"Good! Don't sign anything, absolutely nothing at all. I'm going to take the wheelchair back to the front hall and I'll tell them that I'm your lawyer and I'm taking you out to lunch.

I'll be right back." And he was gone, almost running back the way they had strolled. Joan sat in his car with the windows down and a lovely breeze blowing. He was back in five minutes. "That's done. Now where would you like to go?"

"Somewhere where we can sit outside. It is wonderful being out in the air."

"I can't bear to think of what you've been through! And there I was on a ridiculous cruise ship instead of beside you." They drove with both the windows open and Joan reveled in feeling the breeze on her face and her hair blowing every which way.

"How about we buy sandwiches and go sit by the river in Hudson?"

"That sounds wonderful."

Alejandro parked in front of a café on Warren Street near his old office. After a few minutes he came out carrying a very full paper bag and they continued driving down Warren Street toward the park with picnic tables by the river. Once again Alejandro tucked Joan's arm under his elbow, and with that security she was able to walk on the uneven ground.

They ate thick cheese and tomato sandwiches, drank ice teas and watched the tour boat come into the dock. "Would you like to go on the next excursion on the river? It takes an hour and will start in about ten minutes."

"Did you tell the rehab when I'd be back?"

"I said I had no idea; that we had a lot to discuss."

"And they said okay?"

"Describing myself as your lawyer, do you have one by the way, gives us a lot of discretion."

"No, I don't have a lawyer, not until today. Thank you Alejandro for becoming my lawyer."

"You're welcome. As your lawyer I want to remind you, Do not sign anything without my being there! Nobody, not even your daughter, can make you sign something without your lawyer!"

"I'll remember. Yes, let's go on the excursion." Joan felt brimming over with joy and the desire to be as close as possible to Alejandro, and ready to do anything.

The sky had become grey with clouds that looked heavy with rain. The only other tourists on the boat was a family with four children. It soon became clear that this family knew a lot about the Hudson river and the birds that lived along the cliffs; they excitedly pointed things out to each other. It was thanks to a girl who looked to be thirteen that Alejandro and Joan saw a bald eagle for the first time in their lives.

Alejandro and Joan listened closely to what the family was saying among themselves, as they held hands and stared wordlessly at the water, at the shore, at the sky, at the birds, at the lighthouse in the middle of the river, and once in a while at each other, smiling as happily as the children.

Chapter Forty-nine

Paul's favorite activity as a member of Tom's household was buying groceries. Tom and Janie did a weekly shopping, but when something had been forgotten, or had run out, Paul volunteered to get it. There was a small grocery store a couple of blocks away owned by a Puerto Rican couple. Paul spoke with them in Spanish and they were happy to gather the things he asked for into the tote bag he'd brought with him.

As he tapped his white cane along the sidewalk he liked hearing the voices of the people around him and the music coming from their radios. There was a bench in front of the grocery store and he often sat there for a while before heading back to the apartment. He listened to bits of conversations as the people walked by him. Sometimes when a stranger asked, "Can I help you, Father?" Paul would draw them into a conversation. Women especially felt comfortable sitting beside him on the bench and telling him about their children or grandchildren. At those times Paul felt almost as though he were back home in Mérida.

He still had no idea what he was supposed to be doing in Harlem. He'd offered to help out at his old church. The young priest was friendly but seemed slightly bewildered by the idea that a blind priest could be helpful to him in any way at all.

Two weeks after Seamus's visit Paul received a letter from him.

Dear Father Paul,

Thank you for meeting with me and introducing me to the image of the Virgin of Guadalupe!

I want to ask if you would consider the possibility of coming north to Columbia County, perhaps once a month, to hear confessions from the Latino farm workers who believe they shouldn't receive communion unless they've been to confession.

The priest in Carleton is half Puerto Rican but he's not fluent in Spanish. I asked him what he thought about hearing confession even if he didn't understand what was being said.

"I'm ready to listen," he said. "There are times when things need to be said even if they can't be understood. But giving absolution is another question."

I asked him what he thought of the possibility of your coming here maybe once a month to hear confessions.

"That's a great idea. I'd be delighted to have Father Paul stay with me in the rectory. I would appreciate help in reaching out to the Latinos."

Michael and I would bring you back and forth from the city. We would bring the Latino workers from all over the county to the church in Carleton so you could hear their confessions. Does this sound possible?

Michael has maps to figure out our route to you. And there are at least forty Latino farmworkers and their families who are here year round and would be very grateful if you could come.

I realize, Father Paul, I haven't even asked about your health. I was happy to see you looking so well when I visited. I know I'm asking a great deal and that it's a long shot. You know how grateful I am for everything you've done already, for me and for Michael.

My very best wishes for your health and happiness,

Seamus

Janie read the letter aloud to Paul. After a minute she asked, "Do Catholics still bother with confessions nowadays?"

"Some do. In Mexico many people go to confession each week."

"And up here?"

"Up here, not so much."

"Do you go to confession?"

"Yes, but not every week."

"Maybe you could go up there once and explain to the Latino workers that the rules are different in the north."

"That's a thought," Paul said. "But it might be a good idea to give you and Tom a break from looking after me for a few days a month."

"Paul, we don't look after you; you look after us, blind as you are. You bring such a warmth and peace and joy into the apartment. I don't really have words to tell you how grateful I am that you've joined us here."

"Thank you, Janie," Paul said, embarrassed to realize that he'd been fishing for some sort of reassurance.

Life with Tom and Janie was confounding in some ways. It was the first time that he'd been living as part of the family since he turned nineteen. Now he was seventy two and Tom at seventy-five had taken him on as a project for his retirement years. Paul hated being Tom's project! But he hoped that by humbling himself into accepting the role, they could come to peace with the past. He also hated knowing that a second perhaps lethal stroke was haunting his footsteps!

After hearing Seamus's letter, Paul prayed in gratitude for the possibility of regular trips to Carleton, where he could be active as a priest again! Then he thought that perhaps he could spend weekdays in Carleton with the young priest. He could teach him Spanish, perhaps help out with weekday Mass and marriage preparations. He could come to the city on the weekends to be Tom's project two days out of the week rather than five.

That afternoon he asked Janie to write his response to Seamus.

Dear Seamus,
I enjoyed our meeting very much. I like the idea of helping your

priest with hearing confessions and in any other way. I am eager to serve as a priest again in any capacity.

Best wishes, and God bless,

Father Paul

Chapter Fifty

Since Seamus no longer had an office upstairs at Treehouse Books, he needed to come up with reasons to visit the store so he could spend time with Maggie. Sometimes he said he was looking for a specific book; sometimes he planned a meeting with Michael.

After using these reasons too often, he decided he could simply invite her out for supper in Hudson, and so he did.

"Tonight? That sounds lovely. I have errands to do in Hudson, so I'll meet you there."

She was waiting for him in front of the restaurant when he arrived. "Have you been waiting long?"

"No, I just got here. I stopped in at my competition down a couple of blocks. They have both old and new books and I'm considering imitating them."

"Imitating them?"

"Yes, making an arrangement with a distributor to sell new best sellers."

"Is Treehouse not doing well? You always look busy."

"It's the bookstore owners from New York and Boston that keep me afloat. They make large purchases to resell in the cities. My favorite customers are my neighbors, but many of them bring back the books they bought the month before for credit toward their next purchases. I earn pennies that way. If I sold new books at full price, I would make a profit when they came back used."

This was the first time Maggie had ever confided in Seamus about her finances. "Let's go in." Seamus said, holding open the heavy red door. They walked past the bar and into the dining room. Through a sliding glass door they went out onto the patio in the back. There were trees there, and the patio was surrounded by a high wooden fence which made it feel very private. The sky slowly became dark, and the large candle on their table glowed more and more brightly.

Seamus thought Maggie astoundingly beautiful as she sipped her wine and ate linguine with shrimp. He dug into fish and chips, and a beer on tap. They talked about Michael's desire to go to college in New York City. When Michael's parents asked Maggie if he could live with her so they could concentrate on their careers in India, he had been thirteen, and very shy. He wanted to be homeschooled. Maggie asked Seamus for help with teaching Michael, and they both found the experience exhilarating. Maggie taught him English Literature and History. Seamus took on everything else, which meant that Seamus had to study up on things he knew nothing about. Michael and he learned those things together giving each other lectures on subjects they'd researched independently.

"And he did okay!" Seamus bragged, "getting into NYU."

"Yes, Seamus, I can't thank you enough."

"I enjoyed every minute of it. How about some chocolate cake for dessert."

"Good idea," Maggie agreed with a smile.

They shared the cake, dipping their forks into the same piece, which Seamus found surprisingly intimate. They also ordered espresso. Seamus would have enjoyed another beer but he wanted to keep his head clear.

After paying the tab, he asked if Maggie would like to take a walk. "I think we'd better," she said.

The night was cool and clear, the sky brilliant with stars. The stores on Warren Street were closed, but there were a few lights here and there from restaurants and bars. They headed downhill toward the Hudson River. Seamus wanted very much to take Maggie's hand, but feared she might pull away in surprise

After they walked a few blocks in silence, Maggie said, "This has been a lovely evening. Thank you so much."

"You're most welcome," Seamus said, wishing he knew how to tell her how much he was enjoying it.

"Perhaps we should turn around," Maggie said, after more silence. "I'm beginning to get cold."

"Do you remember when I went to visit Boston the first time?" Seamus said ignoring her words.

"Yes, you went to see your friend Father Gerald."

"I also went to the cemetery where Rose is buried."

Maggie didn't say anything, but it seemed to Seamus that she shivered a little. Finally, after a long pause, Seamus said, "There's been a change..." There was no way he could say more.

"What sort of change?" Maggie asked.

When he didn't respond for another half block, she asked, "Do you want to tell me about the change?"

The word that Seamus said to himself was *desperately.* But what he said aloud was, "Yes."

They walked on in silence. The ball was in Seamus's court but he had no idea how to begin. Finally Maggie said, "Maybe we should start back to the car. I'm getting cold."

"No," Seamus said. It was now or never to tell her, but he still had no words.

"Well then you'll have to put your arm around me," Maggie said matter of factly "because I'm getting cold."

Seamus put his arm around her shoulders. His tongue loosened as he felt her warm body under his arm and he said, "How about we go to my apartment and warm up?"

"Okay."

Seamus lived on Union Street which ran parallel to Warren. It was a residential street and therefore almost completely dark as they walked over to it and continued down toward the river. Seamus led Maggie around to the side door of a big Victorian and then slowly up the two flights of back stairs, and then the newer narrow staircase with bannisters that had been put in for easy access to the attic. His landlady had suggested they use different stairs to give each other privacy.

His apartment was in the attic; it was one large room with a kitchen against one wall and a tiny bathroom. There were three large skylights which, before he turned the lights on, were filled with the stars and moon. "Oh turn the lights off, please," Maggie said. "Isn't that beautiful!"

Seamus turned off the light and led Maggie to the sofa where they sat and leaned back against the pillows to stare up at the sky. After a while Maggie asked into the darkness, "Can you tell me about the change now?"

"Yes," Seamus said. "I think I can." After a few deep breaths he continued, "One of the reasons I'm so fond of Michael, one of the many reasons, is that when things were difficult for you and Michael in New Delhi, you sent for me. I had the great joy of being with you both day and night for almost a month. During that time I fell head over heels in love with you. I felt as though I'd been given a new family, and I was filled to the brim..." he couldn't finish the sentence.

Maggie put her hand in his but didn't say anything.

"When we returned to the States I was drawn back into my past. I remembered my vow to love Rose until the day I died. That vow made me cringe with guilt at what I was feeling for you."

As Seamus said that, Maggie tried to let go of his hand, but he held on tight and continued, "I'm not sure what finally knocked some sense into me. Perhaps it's the Boston house becoming a refuge. Perhaps it's getting to know the farm workers who work here to support their families, even though their work prevents them from going home for years on end. Or it may be that Rose has been lobbing snowballs at me from across the River Styx to get my attention. But finally, finally Maggie dearest, I realize that love is infinitely available, and all we can do is add to it."

Maggie didn't say anything but they continued to hold hands. After a few moments he went on, "I've realized something else as well. By telling myself that my vow to Rose cut off the possibility of my loving you, I was in fact shielding myself from the humiliation of being a man with a stump that no right-minded woman would ever consider."

"Ah," Maggie finally said, "You've discovered that I'm not right minded."

"I've discovered the courage to hope that you might consider the possibility of accepting undying love from an infinitely stupid old man with one foot."

"I think I just might," Maggie said matter of factly.

"Oh my God." Seamus leaned closer to find her face in the dark and then her lips. When Maggie kissed him back, he felt as though they'd flown out through the skylights into the night sky where the stars and the moon were circling around them.

Chapter Fifty-one

"Oh my God, Maggie, you're so beautiful!" Burst from Seamus as he handed her a cup of coffee the next morning."

"And you, my dear, could compete with Jimmy Stewart."

Seamus had worried that Maggie would be put off when she actually saw his stump, but that hadn't happened. He felt about nineteen, as though he were about to begin life all over again. "Shall we get married today?"

"Married?"

"Don't you want to? I mean now that... Don't you want to get married and make it alright?"

"Seamus, dearest, everything is alright right now. No, I don't and never will want to get married. I've been married and I disliked the experience intensely."

"But...."

"Seamus, everything is good just as it is, more than good. Let's just enjoy it."

They were silent for a while sipping coffee, eating scrambled eggs and english muffins, and smiling at each other. Seamus felt happy right down to the toes of his one foot.

After a while of silently reveling, he thought of Michael. Was Michael worrying about Maggie not coming home?

"I called Michael last night after you fell asleep," Maggie said.

Seamus loved knowing that she could read his mind. "What did you tell him?"

"That I was spending the night with you. Are you concerned about my reputation?"

That stopped Seamus in his tracks. The answer was yes. He was concerned about her reputation, and his own. Not his outward reputation, but his conscience. He'd never before made love to anyone beside Rose. He was still a little in shock about what he'd done. Maggie seemed to read his thoughts as she asked, "Are you concerned about what Father Brennan would think?"

Seamus sat stock still, his coffee cup lifted but not drunk from, as he asked himself that question. He imagined telling Gerald about last night, and he waited for a moment to hear his response.... To his surprise and huge relief he heard Gerald begin to chuckle and then to laugh outright. Seamus breathed deeply, sipped his coffee, and sat more comfortably on his chair. "I think he'll be all right with it," he told Maggie.

After breakfast they walked uptown to get Maggie's car, and she took off to open Treehouse Books. As he walked back to the apartment, Seamus decided to invite Caitlin and Malika out for supper. He and Caitlin had never talked about the possibility of his falling in love again after her mother's death. It seemed important that he should at least hint to her what had happened. Seamus was fearful that she might feel he was betraying her mother. In any case Caitlin was certainly the first person who should be told.

Seamus called her as soon as he got home.

"We have a dress rehearsal tonight, Dad, "The Zoo Story". Would you like to come watch it? The rehearsal's at six. After that the three of us could get supper in Carleton."

"Yes, I'd like that. I'll see you at 6:00."

The play was one act. A man sat on a bench in Central Park. Another man sat down beside him and said he was coming from the zoo. By a combination of verbal curve balls, jabs, and punches below the belt, one of the strangers goaded the other into murdering him. As a policeman, who had continuously tried, and sometimes succeeded, in preventing violence with his words, Seamus found this play infuriating.

It was late when the rehearsal was over, and they went to a bar that served hamburgers. They sat on three stools around a high round table. Malika was wearing a close-fitting red dress that showed her shapely legs when she sat on the stool. Caitlin was wearing her almost perpetual baggy bluejeans and a large yellow tee-shirt on which was printed in red Be Aware.

Seamus stared at these young women. He was filled with pride at their beauty and their wonderfulness.

Once they had ordered he said, "I wonder what Maggie would think of that play."

"You should bring her! She's the one who turned me on to Albee," Caitlin said.

"Well, maybe I will," Seamus said. "Maggie and I have become very good friends." He emphasized the word, "very" wanting to tell them what he thought they should know without actually telling them anything, in case it would upset Caitlin too much.

"Well, it's about time," Caitlin said with a smile.

"What do you mean?"

"You've been in love with her for years. What took you so long?"

"But I never..."

"Dad," she interrupted him, "I'm your daughter. The fact that you don't talk about your feelings doesn't get in the way of my knowing them. The way you look at her, the way you lean toward her, the way your eyes sparkle when you talk about her; you're like my friend's three year old who thinks he's hidden when he's behind a sunflower. Your feelings are always showing to me."

It had not occurred to Seamus that Caitlin cared about him in that way. He didn't know what to say.

"What she means," Malika filled in the pause, "is congratulations! And I want to add that we're both very happy for you."

To be absolutely sure that he didn't tear up in front of the girls, Seamus quickly got off the stool and walked over to the bar to order three more beers. By the time they were poured,

and he'd carried them back to the table, he was almost himself
again.

Chapter Fifty-two

Dear Father Paul,

It looks as though I jumped the gun when I invited you here to hear confessions.

The priest in Carleton is being moved, and it turns out the interim priest is bilingual. I thank you so much for being willing, and I very much look forward to seeing you again.

All best wishes,

Seamus

When Janie read that note aloud, Paul realized how much he'd been counting on spending weekends in Carleton. He desperately needed breaks from being shut up with Tom day in and day out.

The cardiologist had told him that another stroke could come at any time, that he should 'take things easy.' Paul wondered if the doctor had told Tom something else, because Tom acted as though he were wrapping Paul up in a shroud of over protection and isolation to ready him for his coffin!

Despite the warm sunny weather and the leafing out of the trees that they could watch from their windows, there was no joy in the apartment. Tom's knee hurt continuously. He grumbled that Janie was nagging him when she suggested he have the operation to get a new knee joint. Instead, he asked Paul to rub his knee with a cream that advertised itself as "able to soak up the pain so you don't have to feel it." Paul rubbed Tom's knee every few hours to no avail, which made Tom more desperate and more angry. Tom's pain clouded and darkened everything: cooking, eating together; even watching television was interrupted by loud grunts as Tom shifted his position.

Paul prayed for patience. He prayed for discernment. *What should I be doing?* He asked again and again.

Finally, one Saturday night, the answer came. While Paul was kneeling in prayer by his bed, he overheard a conversation between Tom and Janie through the thin wall between their bedrooms. "There's no way I can get a knee replacement!" Tom shouted with adamantine conviction. "Paul needs me to take care of him!"

Paul's fury at Tom's using him as an excuse, as he often had when Paul was a child, made him end his prayers abruptly, grab his jacket, leave his bedroom, and then at the front door grab his cane and leave the apartment. It was about nine o'clock and he hadn't thought to find his wallet. He hadn't thought of anything but to get some air. Once he was outside though, he knew what he needed to do. But without money in his pocket he needed help in order to do it.

He walked tapping wildly, not actually counting his steps or the corners he was turning, but when he heard the church organ he knew where he was. The door was unlocked and he followed the music to the organ itself. He asked the priest who was playing, if he could make a long distance call to Mexico.

It was Jorge himself who answered at the rectory. "I've been trying to reach you." he said in Spanish. "Didn't you get my messages?"

Before Paul could ask, 'what messages?' Jorge said, "Please come home. I am not well. Please come!"

Tom was so angry about Paul's decision to leave for Mexico that Paul could feel Tom's body vibrate with the desire to shake him or knock him senseless. Through the thin walls Paul could hear Janie explain to Tom how important it was to leave Paul free to follow his own path, no matter how unreasonable and foolishly risky it might be.

Paul heard Tom shout, "You don't understand. He's my brother. He's my younger brother. He's blind. He's frail. I'm supposed to take care of him. If Dad knew that I was letting Paul go and die in another country he'd turn over in his grave…. No he wouldn't, he'd take off his belt and beat some sense into me. You don't let your blind kid brother jump off a cliff like that. That's not how our family lives!"

"Sweetheart, your blind kid brother is seventy-two. He may not have long to live. Now is the time to leave him free to follow his own desires. There's nothing you can do to protect him from dying either here or in Mexico. He'll be surrounded by religious people there and he'll be doing what he believes in, what he's believed in since he was a teenager. It seems to me that's a wonderful way to approach death."

"And what about me? I can't even help my kid brother? What about me and the end of my life?"

"Tom, you've been a hero throughout your life. So hard working, so loving, such a good husband, father, grandfather. There's nobody in the world like you."

After that there was silence. Paul was filled with gratitude toward Janie as he packed his suitcase with the clothes she had washed and ironed for him. He put in the small water-smoothed stone that Michael had given him when they separated. "It's from the waterfall at Bash Bish. I went back there to find it for you."

The next morning Janie had to leave for work early. She gave Paul a long hug and said, "Whatever happens we've got your back."

"Bless you, dear Janie," Paul said, "and thank you for giving Tom such a wonderful life. I love seeing you so happy together."

"No thanks to you," Tom said gruffly.

"You're forgetting that you met Janie at a jazz club where I was playing and you were watching out for me."

Tom didn't say anything — Janie went over to Tom and kissed him hard on the mouth. "I'll see you later, Handsome.

Take care, Paul," and she was gone.

"I'm coming to the bus stop with you."

"Great," Paul said, knowing better than to argue.

"And I'd like to make an exchange with you."

"What do you mean?"

Tom put into Paul's hand a cane. After a minute Paul realized it was the cane Tom had been using since his knee acted up. "I'd like you to use this. Not only because it's more sturdy than yours, but I'd like you to have in your hand something that's been in my hand for more than a year. I covered it with white tape so it's very clear that you're using it because you're blind. It won't tap as loudly because it has a piece of rubber over the tip, but that means that it won't slip as easily. It will mean a lot to me, Paul, if you'll say you'll use it."

"Of course I will, Tom. Thank you." Tom then picked up Paul's suitcase and they headed for the bus stop. They waited with a small group of people at 125th street for the bus to LaGuardia airport. Nobody in the group seemed to have much to say to each other, but Tom kept his hand on Paul's shoulder the twenty minutes or so that they waited. When the bus came Tom hugged Paul hard. As they kissed each other on the cheek, Paul felt Tom's tears. "I'll call," Paul said.

"You damn well better," Tom replied as he gave Paul a shove up onto the bus and handed him his suitcase.

Chapter Fifty-three

The first thing Paul noticed in Mérida was the wonderful warmth. He'd been half frozen in New York for so long that he was no longer aware of it. Even in the airport, his body relaxed and he could feel his shoulders drop out of their huddled position. A porter approached him speaking in Spanish, "Can I help you Father? Are you looking for Customs?"

"Yes, I am, thank you." Paul soon realized that the porter must have taken him to the beginning of the line because he was through Customs in minutes. Then the porter led him to a line of waiting taxis. "I think I'll wait here for a few minutes," Paul told him. "It may be that someone will be coming to pick me up."

"Then, Father, I suggest you stand back here a few steps so people will know that you're not in line." Once again he'd been put at the front of the line although he'd heard nobody complain.

"Welcome home, Father," Paul heard a familiar voice say in Spanish. And then he felt Sister Maria's hand touch his shoulder. "Sister Ana and I are here to bring you home. Please come with me. We are filled with gratitude for your return."

Sister Maria and Sister Ana sat in the front seat after they made sure Paul was comfortable in the back seat with his cane and suitcase. At the rectory door he left the suitcase and hurried to Jorge's bedroom which was next door to the room he had lived in for decades. He knew that Jorge's room was like his own, with a washstand, a ceramic bowl, a pitcher, a row of pegs for clothes, a small table and chair, and a shelf above them for books.

Jorge was awake and greeted Paul softly happily. Paul heard him slowly sit up in bed. Paul felt for Jorge's pillows to fit them behind him. "Is that comfortable?" he asked in Spanish.

"Your coming makes everything comfortable. I'm so grateful that you've arrived in time." After a few moments of silence Jorge asked, "Do you remember in the Cathedral the little closet to the right of the organ where we put spare parts for the organ and other things?"

"I do."

"I think there's a keyboard in there."

"A keyboard?"

"Yes. Perhaps we could sing together."

"I'll go find it." Paul said.

At the door of the rectory Paul felt for his suitcase but it was gone. He knew one of the sisters had taken it to his old room. As he crossed the street to the Cathedral he felt deeply happy to be back. He knew the Cathedral and rectory and this part of Mérida so well, that it was almost as though everything was filled with light and he was seeing his way as he could when he was a child.

Yet something was different and making difficulties. It was Tom's cane. It was all very well to have a piece of rubber at the tip so the cane wouldn't slip, but with his old cane Paul could learn a lot by hearing the tapping of the tip. He could tell wood from cement, hollow from insulated etc. He walked over to the front pew of the Cathedral and sat down. He lifted up the cane and pulled the rubber off the bottom. He put the rubber in his pocket and tapped his way to the closet behind the organ. He reached in, feeling behind various objects that he didn't try to identify, until his hand clutched a keyboard which he carefully drew out.

Back in Jorge's room he put the keyboard on the table and moved the chair so he could sit on it to play. He began to play "De Colores", a song about colors and joy in every aspect of life. Jorge sang with him, but when the song was over he said, "Thank you. I think I need to lie down again. Can you help me?" Paul held Jorge's blankets up so he could slip under them, and then he arranged his pillows behind his head.

"Would you like more music?" Paul asked.

"Yes, please," Jorge whispered. So Paul played one of their favorites, "Pescador de Hombres", a song written from the point of view of a fisherman without possessions who offers himself to follow Jesus and become a fisher of men. They sang it together. Paul lowered his voice to almost a whisper like Jorge's so it was a real duet. After that Jorge mumbled his thanks and said, "Please more." So Paul played the Easter hymn, "Resucitó", but he played it softly instead of with the usual celebratory loudness. Paul meant it for Jorge alone, knowing that he too would rise when the time came.

The sisters arranged to have a bed for Paul moved into Jorge's room. The two beds filled the room and the table and chair were moved out. Only the washstand with its bowl and pitcher remained. Often, during the day and the night, Paul wet the wash cloth and wiped the sweat off of Jorge's brow. Jorge slept a great deal. He had no interest in eating but sometimes sipped a little water when Paul held the glass to his lips. Paul sat on his bed with his back against the wall much of the day. He prayed the liturgy of the hours aloud, and sometimes heard a whispery response from Jorge. He read aloud from the braille Bible especially Jorge's favorite passages from Romans, and the Book of Job. Sister Ana told Paul that Jorge smiled sometimes while he was reading. Paul wished he could see Jorge's face as he traveled on this last journey. He played their favorite hymns softly on the keyboard, but no longer sang the words.

One night Paul woke up hearing Jorge struggle to draw breath. He went to get Sister Maria who was a nurse. "Medicine won't help him breathe," she said. They sat together on Paul's bed. Paul gave Jorge absolution and then he held Jorge's hand as Sister Maria and he prayed. Sometimes they were saying the same prayer, sometimes they were saying different prayers in different languages under their breath. They were wishing Jorge well on this final journey in their own ways. As they prayed, Jorge's breathing slowly became peaceful, and finally there were longer and longer intervals between breaths until there was no breath at all.

Sister Maria gently closed Jorge's eyes. Then she went to tell the others. After a few minutes there were three sisters, a brother, and two priests standing flat against the walls of the small room singing Ave Maria softly in harmony which is what Jorge had asked them to do when the time came.

Paul knew Jorge was at peace. But he longed to pull him back from wherever he'd gone, pull him back into his life again. The halls of the rectory, where they'd lived together for decades, now seemed to echo as though they were empty.

Chapter Fifty-four

Alejandro visited Joan every day. "I have something to show you," he said one morning, "but not until we're outside. Do you want to take a brief ride in that awful wheelchair until we get out of sight?"

"Yes, let's."

At the promontory where they had left the wheelchair on Alejandro's first visit, Joan stood up and took his arm and they strolled like an old-fashioned couple until they came to their favorite view where there were chairs to sit on, and he showed her what he'd brought. It was an announcement for a juried exhibit of paintings in Ipswich, Massachusetts. "You used to live there didn't you?"

"My goodness you have a good memory."

"They're asking artists to send photographs or slides of only one painting. Which one would you choose?"

"I wouldn't choose any. They're talking about real artists."

"Describe 'real.'"

Joan sighed dramatically, but then smiled and leaned over and kissed his cheek.

"Since all they want is a photograph, if they don't choose you, you've lost nothing."

Joan wanted to quote King Lear's speech about nothing

coming from nothing but she couldn't remember it well enough, so instead she said with another dramatic sigh, "Oh, okay."

"Which one will you choose?"

"Angelica. Maybe as a painter herself, she'll bring me luck."

"Do you have a photograph of the painting?"

"No, that's what I mean. They're talking about real artists."

"I see, real means taking photos of what you paint. Listen, Juana, I'm not a bad photographer. "I'll take the photograph and send it in."

Joan grabbed the arms of the chair she was sitting on and carefully stood up straight and tall on her own. Sarah had declared that Joan was being a burden to her family unless she gave up everything she cared about, not only painting, but also walking itself. Sarah was furious that Joan had refused to hand over her apartment keys. "Mom, you're acting like a stubborn old mule! And you're wasting precious money by paying high rent for a place you'll never see again, full of stuff you'll never want!"

Joan reached into her pocket now and pulled out her downstairs and upstairs door keys. She showed them to Alejandro. "You'll need these to get in. I suggest you stay there for a while. Why commute back and forth from the musty basement in New Jersey?"

Alejandro stood up to receive the keys and put them in his

pocket. He smiled at Joan with such tenderness that without any warning even to herself, she reached her arms around his neck and kissed him on the lips. His tenderness quickly changed to desire. Their kisses deepened until they finally leaned back from each other to catch their breath and stare into each other's eyes with surprise and wonder.

During the next weeks Joan worked hard on standing and walking. Mary gave her specific exercises to do on her own. After Joan was able to walk three times around her room without touching anything, Mary took her out into the hall. Highlands had given Joan a cane. "Don't let it touch the floor!" Was Mary's advice. And Joan didn't! The next week, Mary opened the heavy door to the stairwell. This time she put a belt around Joan so that she could keep her upright if she began to fall. Joan held on to the banister and they did three flights of stairs with not one tug on the belt. "Congratulations! You have graduated!" Mary declared.

It was the day Joan graduated that Alejandro brought her a postcard from the Episcopal church in Ipswich, declaring, "We are delighted to include your work in our exhibit. Please deliver your painting three days before the exhibition opens on July Fourth."

"I'm so happy for you!"

Joan was happy too, but wary. She couldn't quite believe that they meant it, so she made difficulties by asking with a whine, "How can we get the painting to Ipswich three days before, and then go back for the exhibit itself?"

"Let's go for a ride," Alejandro said. "I want to suggest something."

"Okay."

Alejandro explained at the desk that he was taking his client out to lunch.

"One minute sir."

"Yes?"

"Mrs. Estrada's daughter called when the two of you were meeting somewhere. She said that she had not contracted you as a lawyer for her mother. She requested that I ask to look at your license and make a copy of it.

"Why certainly."

When she gave him back his license they walked outside and Joan was holding his hand instead of clinging to his elbow. They drove to her apartment in Carleton. "I thought we might have something to eat in the café and then I could help you up the stairs to your apartment and you could pack yourself a suitcase."

"A suitcase?"

"For the trip to Ipswich."

"Why would I need a suitcase?"

"Ah, Juana, I am not doing this well. Let's eat something. Maybe a latte will clear my head and I'll be able to explain my idea."

After the waitress brought their lattes and pieces of rhubarb pie, Joan asked, "So, tell me, why do I need a suitcase?"

"Okay, but first I want to say that our friendship is more important than my suggestion. If my suggestion makes you angry, I hope you can erase it from your mind and we can go on being friends."

"I can't imagine a suggestion that would make us not be friends."

Alejandro reached across the table and took one of Joan's hands. Then he spoke a little quickly as though he wanted to get all the words out before she interrupted him, "How about if we don't go back and forth to Ipswich. How about if we deliver your painting and stay on there for three days and explore Ipswich. You could show me your favorite places. What do you think?"

Joan took her hand away from his, and put both her hands in her pockets. Her heart was thumping as though she were climbing a steep hill. She felt eighteen and eighty at the same time. After a long silence she said, "Our friendship means a lot to me as well. I'd hate to have whatever happens…." She trailed off into silence. When Alejandro didn't say anything, she continued, "Of course it would probably be wonderful, but I'm an old lady and I just don't know…" again she trailed off into silence.

After a couple of minutes Alejandro said, "I agree completely. Let's put our friendship first; then whatever else happens, wonderful or difficult, can simply become part of it."

Joan stared at him, tall and somewhat gaunt, coppery skinned, with a face that often looked melancholy but now seemed lit by the sun, although there was no sun. They stared at each other for a few minutes. "Let's do it," Joan said.

"Yes, let's," he agreed.

"But what about the rehab?"

"That's one reason I wanted to bring you here. Let's see how it feels for you to climb the stairs to your apartment. It seems to me that maybe you no longer need the rehab."

"That's exactly what my physical therapist said. 'You're doing fine,' she said, 'now get out of here and back to your life.'"

"Good for her."

"What about Sarah?"

"Juana dearest do you really want to spend the rest of your life sitting down so that your family won't worry that you might fall?"

Joan put down her coffee cup with a bit of a clunk as she said, "Let's climb those stairs!"

Chapter Fifty-five

It wasn't until Michael stopped looking for a letter from Mexico every day, that a letter finally arrived from Father Paul.

Dear Michael,

Thank you so much for your letters. I am sorry it has taken me so long to respond to them.

My friend, Father Jorge, has passed on. He was peaceful and ready, but I was not. I wanted to wrestle with God, to keep Jorge with me, at least for a while, but it was not to be. Then I became quite ill myself with weakness and fever. It lasted a week or so and I remember very little about that time. When the fever broke it was as though I was waking up after a long sleep. I knew then that all was well with Jorge and that it was time for me to continue his work at the Cathedral.

I've been teaching classes to children wanting to be confirmed in their faith, and I've been listening to confessions, often from people who, like me, are missing Jorge.

So, dear friend, I am very glad to be working again, but at the same time, I miss you and our adventures together. Please tell me how things are with you.

Congratulations on your being accepted at NYU. I will address my future letters to you there when you send me the address. New York City is filled with things you'll enjoy experiencing. I hope you will continue your study of Spanish. Perhaps you could join me here during your vacations? There would be no difficulty finding a family who would welcome a helping hand for a few months.

I must stop now. The kind sister who has been typing this letter as I say it, must get back to her work now.

God bless you, dear Michael. I look forward to hearing from you.

Father Paul

Chapter Fifty-six

On a late afternoon in June that was just beginning to cool off, Maggie and Seamus were sitting together in companionable silence on the bench outside of Treehouse Books. Maggie had been at an estate sale. She had closed the store for the day because she needed Michael's help packing and carrying the books she bought at the sale. Maggie decided to put off unloading the heavy boxes from the car until the next day, and Seamus offered Michael the use of his car to go to the movies with a friend.

Seamus had been at The Globe hammering sets together that Ron was turning into a wonderful landscape for the "nether nether land" of Peter Pan.

Seamus and Maggie held hands as they sat together with their backs against the wall of the store looking at the field across the road. Seamus was feeling contented down to his toes. The phone inside the store began to ring. "Let's let it go," Maggie said. They continued to hold hands as the annoying jangle went on and on and on.

It finally stopped and they breathed deeply again, until the phone upstairs in Seamus's old office began to ring insistently. "I better get that," he said. "It may be an emergency." He let go of her hand and she handed him her keys to the store. He climbed the stairs as fast as he could, panting a bit as he pulled himself up by the banister. He thought that the phone would stop ringing before he could reach it, but it didn't.

It was Malika who didn't notice his panting but said quickly, "We're off to Hudson. Come join us."

"Huh?"

"You're going to be a grandpa, Seamus! We're off to the hospital."

"Oh God! We're coming!" but she had already hung up. Seamus headed for the stairs and began descending as fast as he could, shouting "The baby's coming. The baby's coming. Get your purse."

By the time he was locking the door to the store Maggie came running out of the house, purse in hand.

Maggie drove quickly, until they got closer to Hudson and were immersed into traffic. The parking lot at the hospital was full. "Shall I leave you off at the front door while I look for a spot?"

"No, no, I'll stick with you." They went round the parking lot two more times and then Maggie squeezed into a space that wasn't really meant for parking, and they headed to the front door of the hospital.

Seamus grabbed Maggie's arm as she was about to ask the receptionist where to go. He put his prosthetic foot against the closing door of the elevator.

On the second floor Seamus led her through the familiar

door into the Family Birth Place. At the reception desk they were greeted by a laughing nurse who said as she hung up the phone, "Hello, Seamus, who are you here with?"

"It's my daughter, Caitlin," he whispered, seeming to have lost his voice.

"Room 214" the nurse said quickly, smiling broadly.

Maggie reached the room before he did. The door was closed, and she waited for Seamus to catch up. When he knocked, Malika opened the door. She kissed his cheek, and then Maggie's, but said nothing. Then she opened the door wider. Caitlin was lying in bed holding a baby wrapped in a white blanket. Seamus went closer. Caitlin beamed at him. "He came like a comet. We thought it was going to happen in the car. Isn't he beautiful?"

"He is," Seamus said, not yet having looked at him, engrossed by the beauty of his daughter's face in her joy.

"His name is James."

"James," Seamus repeated. He stared now at the tiny dark-skinned baby and saw reflected in him, his best friend, Rose's brother.

He felt Maggie behind him and got out of the way so she could look at James. To his surprise, Caitlin held James out toward Maggie asking, "Do you want to hold him, Maggie?"

"Caitlin, dearest, I do indeed."

With James in her arms, Maggie looked for a chair. There was a rocking chair in the corner. Malika carefully took James for a minute while Maggie sat down and then handed him to her. After a few moments of everyone watching little James in Maggie's arms, Caitlin pulled herself a little higher in the bed. Malika arranged the pillows behind her so she could sit comfortably and then took her hand. They smiled at each other for a minute and then Caitlin said, "Maggie, Malika and I want to ask you if you'd be willing to be James's godmother."

Seamus stared at Maggie. She was very pale, and then rosy as she began to cry. "Please, Seamus, take him. I don't want to get him wet with my tears."

Seamus quickly reached for him and then stood straight again with his grandson in my arms. He saw that James's eyes looked remarkably like Caitlin's. He heard her say, "So, Maggie, what do you think about being James's godmother?"

He looked back at Maggie who was crying and smiling at the same time. "Yes," she finally said. "Yes, I would love to be James's godmother."

At that moment, James gave a yawn and a wiggle, and Seamus carefully, but rapidly, gave him back to Caitlin. "We'd better go," he said, not sure he was ready to watch Caitlin nurse him. "We'll see you tomorrow," he said as he kissed Caitlin's cheek and then went to the other side of the bed to kiss Malika who stood up and said as she kissed him back, "Good bye, Grandpa."

"Good bye, Sweetheart." He had a moment of remembering how frightened and shocked he'd been when Caitlin fell in love with Malika. Now she was his second beloved daughter. He took both of Maggie's hands to pull her up from the rocking chair.

"See you tomorrow! Love you!" He said to the three of them. He knew that Maggie would have liked to stay on but he hurried her out of the room before Caitlin began to nurse.

As she was being hustled out of the room Maggie looked back and saw Malika holding James, while Caitlin unbuttoned her nightgown preparing to nurse. As Seamus drove them back to the house neither of them said a word.

Seamus had told Maggie about the other James, his colleague, brother-in-law and best friend. James had introduced Seamus to Rose, joined the police force with Seamus, and then died as a young man trying to protect a crowd from a sniper.

Maggie wondered if baby James would be able to relieve Seamus's sadness about his friend's death. As Seamus drove in silence, Maggie felt her shoulders relax, although she hadn't known they were tense. She felt her back lean more comfortably against the car seat, although she hadn't known she was perching on it. Being wanted as a Godmother by Seamus's daughter made her relax somewhere deep inside.

Chapter Fifty-seven

On their way back to the hospital the next morning Maggie asked Seamus to stop in Carleton. She bought cotton yarn, knitting needles, and a pattern for a baby's sweater at the Warm Ewe.

"I'm going to leave you off at the hospital," Seamus told her. "I need to buy some paint for the new set."

"No hurry," Maggie told him. "If the girls need privacy, or I need exercise, I'll go for a walk and meet you back at the hospital." Treehouse Books was closed for the day in celebration.

"Maggie!" was Caitlin's warm greeting as Maggie slowly opened the door to her room. Caitlin was sitting up in bed nursing James, who seemed to be enjoying himself thoroughly. In fact they both did. Caitlin's face seemed almost beatific with happiness.

Maggie sat down in the rocking chair, with her bag of knitting stuff, and asked, "Where's Malika?"

"She's auditioning new actors." As Caitlin said that, she put James expertly against her chest and burped him gently. Then she moved her nightgown around and settled him on her other breast. After a few minutes when all they could hear was James's sucking, and nurses and doctors talking on the other side of the door, Caitlin said, "When I started having crushes on girls I thought I would never have this experience. I even considered pretending to love some guy in order to have children. But when a boy tried to kiss me, I was so repulsed that I realized that was not going to happen. But here we are, me and Malika with a beautiful son."

"Yes indeed," Maggie said as she began putting stitches on a slim knitting needle.

After a minute Caitlin continued. "I know that Dad would have preferred that we adopt."

"You know your dad likes to follow the church's teachings whenever possible." This was the first time Caitlin and Maggie had ever talked about Seamus.

"I know. And the church prefers adoption to what we did, but of course what we did wasn't even possible years ago." After a few minutes of Caitlin burping James, and Maggie counting stitches, Caitlin went on. "The thing is, I was adopted. My folks were wonderful parents and I'm completely grateful, but I still wonder who my birth parents were and why they didn't want me. Malika says we should look into it someday when we're at leisure, which probably means never. Anyway I wanted our child to have no question about how much he was loved by the parents who gave birth to him."

"Have you told Seamus about your reasons?"

"No, but I was thinking that if the question comes up, you

might explain it to him. I think you and Father Gerald between you, in different ways of course, keep Dad happily sane, despite his being so conservative in terms of religion."

"You, Malika and James are making your dad overflow with happiness."

Instead of responding Caitlin settled James on her lap where he fell asleep. Maggie went back to her knitting until Caitlin without warning asked, "Are you and Dad getting married soon? Talking about following the Church's teachings whenever possible."

Maggie was surprised into silence. Before words came to her, Caitlin continued, "I don't believe Dad's ever had a lover before. I would have thought that he would have insisted on tying the knot first."

Maggie's stomach cramped painfully realizing for the first time what a sacrifice she was asking of Seamus.

"I was married once," She told Caitlin. "Frank used to hit me. I'd be in the middle of telling him something, and then, pow! When I was on the floor cringing and crying, he would lower himself to the floor beside me. 'Why do you make me do this?' he would ask pathetically. 'Why can't you be the kind of wife a man can be proud of? Look what you're turning me into?'"

"'I'm sorry. I'll try harder,' I would say, hoping that would make the beating stop, at least for a while. When he first started to hit me, I'd ask, 'What did I do wrong?' Those beatings went on forever as though my stupidity was driving him insane."

After a sigh, Maggie continued, "All that ended almost forty years ago. One evening as I was getting ready for bed, I heard five year old Frankie shout for me and three year old Hannah scream. I ran into their room and saw Frank slap Hannah hard across her little face.

"The next day while Frank was at work, Hannah, Frankie and I took the train to St. Paul, Minnesota. We carried nothing with us because I needed my hands free to hold tightly onto theirs. My parents met us at the station, and we were safe. Since then your dad is the first man I've ever felt comfortable being alone with. I've been hiding from Frank all these years. In order to obtain a divorce I'd have to let him know where I am."

"Does Dad know about this?"

"No, you're the only one, now that my parents have died."

"Thank you for telling me."

After a long silence Maggie asked, "Would you like me to take James?"

"Yes, please. I think I have to lie down."

Maggie put her knitting back in the bag and walked over to the bed to pick up James from Caitlin's lap and bring him back to the rocking chair. Caitlin lay down under the covers, turned over on her side, and was asleep in minutes. Maggie rocked with James humming a lullaby under her breath, and soon he was fast asleep as well. She looked around the room's sunny yellow walls with large colorful prints. One showed children building a sand castle on a beach. Another was of a mother and child sitting in the long grass of a meadow gathering wild flowers, and the third was of older children doing acrobatics on a jungle gym in a city park. Maggie enjoyed immensely the warmth and weight of James on her lap. She leaned back against the cushion of the rocking chair and smiled in the freedom that telling her secret had created.

Chapter Fifty-eight

Neither Joan nor Alejandro could fit the portrait of Angelica into their car, so Alejandro rented a Ford SUV for the week. "I like the idea of setting off on an adventure in a vehicle that's new to both of us," he said as they sped east on Rte 90.

"Me too." It had been a whirlwind two weeks. After finding that she could indeed climb the stairs to her apartment, Joan had signed herself out of the rehab and Alejandro moved back to his granddaughter's basement apartment in New Jersey on the same day.

"I'll see you in two weeks" he'd said. "Enjoy!"

And Joan had enjoyed herself immensely. Her first outing was to the art supply store and then she started work on a portrait of her father. Her memory of him was vague but intense. He'd died of a heart attack when she was fifteen and throughout her childhood she'd longed for him.

Now in her portrait he was walking towards her through a field of high grasses and wildflowers. Behind the field was a mountain ridge. He looked as though he had come down from the mountains to have a conversation and perhaps an adventure with whomever was staring at the portrait.

The Ipswich exhibition and sale was being held downstairs in an historic Episcopal church that needed a new roof. The letter from the exhibition committee asked that each of the artists agree to give half of their sales earnings toward this endeavor.

Joan had not noticed that part of the letter when it arrived, so she'd given no thought to the possibility of selling the portrait. When she and Alejandro handed the portrait of Angelica over, the volunteers accepted it with polite enthusiasm and asked for a title and a price for the catalogue.

Joan thought the title would be easy, but soon realized she didn't want to bandy about with Angelica's name. After a couple of minutes she said, "Barefoot Woman Wearing a Hat." The price was a different problem. It was too late to explain that she had not thought of selling it, so instead she said "A thousand dollars," more or less as a joke. The volunteers politely kept their expressions neutral, and she and Alejandro hurried to leave the basement of the church and get into the air.

They turned down Argilla Road toward the beach, and almost immediately saw a sign saying, "Bed, Breakfast, and Lunch" in front of a white farmhouse, next to a red barn. They parked next to a number of other cars and trucks, and went in. To the left was a counter behind which an elderly man greeted them, "Hello friends, are you here for lunch or are you looking for a room?"

"Are you still serving lunch?" Alejandro asked.

"We certainly are. Go on in there," the man said pointing across the hall to an open door. "My son-in-law is the cook today. I recommend his clam fritters."

"Thank you," Joan said, and they walked through the door into a large sunny room with tall windows where twenty or thirty people were eating at small tables.

After a delicious lunch of clam fritters with home-made hollandaise sauce, and beans and beets from the garden behind the house, they returned to the front counter that was now being manned by a teenager.

"We're thinking of spending the night. Could we look at one of your rooms?" Alejandro asked.

"Of course. Grandpa will be back in a few minutes and then I'll show you."

The room was lovely. It was in the back of the house with two large windows looking out on the fields. The windows were wide open and the room was filled with the smells of summer. The bed was a four poster and was covered by a white quilt with bright yellow flowers embroidered at each corner. They smiled shyly at each other and then went downstairs to claim the room for four days.

They continued driving down Argilla Road until it ended at a beach's parking lot. They followed the boardwalk path over the dunes and then down onto the beach where they took off their shoes and began walking on the sand. Joan felt that her feet and legs were being given a healing massage.

Carrying their shoes they walked to the edge of the waves. The waves curled up and over themselves before breaking into foamy fragments that coalesced and became smooth again. Seagulls and sand- pipers accompanied them as they walked. The sandpipers followed each wave as it slid up onto the sand. Then as the remnants of the wave slid back into the ocean, the sandpipers pecked at the newly wet sand looking for food.

Joan and Alejandro walked until they arrived at large boulders that were creating tide pools in the sand. They climbed up onto one of the boulders and stared down into the pool to look for creatures. As their eyes became accustomed to the reflecting sunlight, Joan saw two hermit crabs and Alejandro pointed out a starfish. Then Joan leaned over too far and slid into the pool. Alejandro quickly jumped in beside her to make sure she wasn't hurt. They sat in the water laughing heartily and began to splash each other like children.

When they were both soaked through, Alejandro stood up and reached for Joan's hands to pull her up as well. They found their shoes and started walking back towards the boardwalk path. The sun had gone behind the clouds and their wet clothes clung.

There was nobody at the counter of "Bed, Breakfast and Lunch." Joan and Alejandro climbed the stairs to their room as quickly and quietly as possible, like children not wanting to be caught. Once in the room, getting out of their wet clothes and under the covers of the four poster took about a minute.

And then time and place and everything else were completely forgotten.

Chapter Fifty-nine

By the day of the art exhibit, Alejandro and Joan were suntanned and rosy cheeked from long walks on the beach and visits to nearby towns. They'd been to Gloucester, to see the fishing boats come in, to Salem, to see where the witch trials took place, and to Manchester by the Sea, to walk along "Singing Beach" and make strange sounds with their feet.

The church basement was filled to overflowing. Joan stared at a painting of a fisherman casting a line into a stream, and wondered what it would be like to paint people out of doors while they were active.

Alejandro put his hand on her shoulder. "I have something to show you," he said. The feel of his hand made Joan so happy she hardly cared what he wanted her to see. She followed him nonchalantly until she realized he was taking her to "Barefoot Woman Wearing a Hat." When they got closer she saw the red dot on its label. Her painting had sold!

The next day as Alejandro drove them back to Carleton, they talked about the future. "What if I keep the house in Hudson, and you move in with me; we'll have your apartment as your studio?"

"I think I'd feel like an intruder in your house."

"Would you like me to move in with you?"

"No, you'd hate the smells of the oil paints and the turpentine! I can bear them because I love painting so much. What do you love doing?"

"Traveling. Beth never wanted to leave Hudson. I've longed to explore South America. I have family there I've never met."

"I have family in Nicaragua whom I'd love you to meet. Perhaps we should buy an RV and head south."

"What about your painting?"

"Years ago my granddaughter and I spent the summer painting every day at Ipswich beach. It was a wonderful experience. If we travel this fall, I'll paint a journal of our trip. When we come back we can figure out what we want to do next.

"That sounds like a honeymoon."

Oh no, Joan thought, *Does he think I'm asking him to marry me?* "I didn't mean it that way," she quickly said.

Alejandro pulled the car to the side of the road and stopped. "Juana dearest..."

He's going to tell me it's too soon. He and his children are still in mourning. He's going to say....

Alejandro unhitched his seatbelt, turned toward Joan and took both her hands in his. "Will you marry me?"

The question was so simple that it flew straight to her heart, evading her doubts. The answer became simple too.

"Yes!" she said, knowing that all was well.

Alejandro kissed her slowly and gently, as though it were for the first time. They smiled at each other in the silence that seemed filled with music.

Chapter Sixty

Jorge was in Paul's thoughts every day. Paul sometimes had long imaginary conversations with him when he walked along the tree-shaded Paseo de Montejo. The sidewalks there were wide enough so people had no difficulty avoiding him when they heard his cane tapping.

Paul had been asked to take on Jorge's duty of hearing confessions. They were often about how the parishioners were missing Father Jorge, "He gave me such good advice but I didn't follow it. Oh Father forgive me for being such an idiot!"

Paul was also teaching Jorge's confirmation classes where the children were eager to tell him, "Father Jorge told the story in a different way. Why did he have to die?"

Sometimes Paul would sit on a bench along the Paseo and complain to Jorge, "I'm walking in your footsteps instead of my own! What should I be doing?" Paul would then listen for advice from his friend, but instead of hearing advice he'd often hear children gather round him and then some of them would climb up on the bench to be nearer. They told Paul what was happening in school or in daycare, and what was happening with their favorite sports teams. They tended to all speak at once and it took a while to hear each child out. When they'd said their fill, they asked for his blessing and jumped off the bench and went their way.

Sometimes adults would greet him and ask if they could speak with him briefly, or ask if they could do anything for him, or they would tell Paul how much they were missing Father Jorge.

It was during one of these conversations that Paul finally had an inkling that Jorge might be trying to get through to him. Sister Ana, a colleague from the Cathedral, sat down beside him one afternoon and said, "Father, do you know how many blind children come to Mass?"

"Blind children?"

"Yes,"

"I don't know."

"How about deaf children?"

"I don't know that either?"

"A mother just spoke to me, in confidence, that she has a three-year old daughter who she keeps at home because she's deaf. The subject came up by chance. We were talking about her desire to learn English and I told her that my second language was Mexican Sign Language."

"Mexican Sign Language?"

"Yes I have a brother who was born deaf, and my mother insisted that we all become fluent in sign language. This lady asked me a lot of questions, and then she told me about her daughter."

"I never thought about the fact that nobody introduces me to their blind children. Sister Ana, do you think there are blind children as well as deaf being kept at home?"

"I think it's very possible."

"Let's go."

"Where?"

"Do you know where the lady with deaf child lives?"

"Yes."

"Let's start by visiting her."

Within six weeks, just by asking questions of a great many people, they found the whereabouts of two deaf children ages three and eight and three blind children, ages four and nine and eleven. They fixed up a room in the rectory as a classroom. The children came with their parents. The families with deaf children came two days a week. Sister Ana taught the children and their parents Mexican Sign Language.

On alternate days Paul taught the blind children and their parents how to read and write in braille. He bought a slate and stylus for each family so they could practice at home, and he told them about a store in Mexico City that sold books in braille. He also brought into the classroom the keyboard that had been in Jorge's room, and gave the children piano lessons.

The number of children increased as word spread, and a monk and two nuns joined them as teachers. It was the monk, who had been a musician in his earlier life, who suggested that on the fifth day of the week they could invite families of both the deaf and the blind to come together to learn how to create an orchestra. He borrowed instruments from friends, and in a few months the deaf children were keeping the beat on the drums and tambourines, and the blind children were playing bamboo flutes, guitars and the keyboard.

Paul asked the Bishop if they could give a performance of this orchestra on a Saturday afternoon. "Some of these children have been hidden away in their homes for years," Paul told him. "I think it would mean a lot to them and to their families if they could experience performing in front of friends and strangers."

The Bishop agreed.

On the afternoon of the performance, Paul was sitting in a front pew listening to the orchestra tune up. The children were helping each with gestures as well as words. The audience was beginning to file in behind Paul, many of them relatives of the musicians. Some of them patted Paul on the shoulder and leaned down to whisper into his ear things like: "My son has become a really good drummer; "My daughter is teaching her friends sign language."

Thank you, Jorge, Paul said silently.

You're welcome, my friend, God bless.

Chapter Sixty-one

Seamus entered Maggie's kitchen after early Mass looking despondent and angry. When she asked what was wrong he almost shouted at her, "The priest refuses to baptize the son of a two-mother family. And he won't let Gerald do it in his church!"

"Should we all drive out to Boston so Father Gerald can do it there?"

"I think that's too far." Seamus poured himself a cup of coffee and took a few sips, and then he looked around Maggie's combination of living room and kitchen and asked in a more hopeful tone of voice, "Maggie, what would you think about having the baptism right here?"

"Here?"

"Yes, this is a lovely room."

"Doesn't it have to be in a church?"

"I don't think so. I can ask Gerald."

"Do you have any idea how many people will come?"

"Caitlin told me they'd be happy to have it just the family. So five of us plus Gerald and James himself."

"That sounds feasible. Why don't you call Gerald and see what he says. Perhaps if it's a beautiful day, we could do it outside. Could you ask him if that would be a possibility?"

While Seamus was calling, Maggie took her second cup of coffee and went outside followed by Olaf, to look for a possible place to hold the ceremony. She loved the way Seamus had included her in 'the family.' She walked around behind the house where she and Michael had been gardening. Michael wanted fresh herbs and so had dug up a bed for them. Then he'd made a larger bed for arugula and different kinds of lettuce. Maggie planted clumps of daffodils and daylilies. The daffodils had bloomed and withered but the daylilies were abundant. Near them was a flat enough area of grass where she decided that about a dozen people could comfortably stand around a table with a beautiful basin that she would have to find or borrow from someone.

Seamus came looking for her. "Gerald says he can come a week from Monday for the ceremony, and then he'll spend the night with me in Hudson. All he needs is a bowl of water, and he says doing it outdoors would be fine as long as it's warm enough, because James will be naked and briefly wet."

"That's wonderful. I hope the sun will shine for us."

It did. Michael and Maggie set the card table up on the flattest area they could find. They dug the bottoms of the legs into the ground. Maggie covered the table with a pale yellow silk shawl that had once belonged to her grandmother. She'd found a large earthenware bowl at an antique store in Hudson. She was going to leave that in the kitchen until it was time to fill it, but Michael said, "Why don't we fill it now, bring it out here and let it sit in the sun to get warm?" It was a good idea, and they did just that.

Maggie and Michael made a variety of sandwiches and chilled two bottles of champagne. Everyone arrived together in festive colorful clothes looking like new plants coming out of the earth, drawn by the sunshine and warmth, the invincible magnetism of summer.

They gathered around the table and Father Gerald blessed the bowl of water. Then he asked Caitlin, "Would you like James to have a dip in the bowl since Maggie has found such a beautiful one? Or would you rather he have drops of water on his forehead."

Malika put her finger in the water and touched Caitlin's arm. "A dip in the bowl" they said in unison.

Father Gerald prayed for James and for his mothers, and for his grandfather, and godmother, as Malika undressed James. Once he was naked, Father Gerald rolled his sleeves up, prayed over him and then took him from Malika's arms and gently lowered him into the bowl. Maggie could see James's body relaxing completely as the sun-warmed water covered his tummy. He seemed to wave to everybody as Father Gerald prayed and then lifted him up and gently passed him to Caitlin who held Maggie's big white bath towel open to receive him. Everyone clapped and hugged and kissed both the parents and their baby. Michael carefully carried the bowl back to the kitchen and brought out the refreshments. Seamus opened the champagne to much applause and everyone dug in.

After James and his mothers had gone home, Seamus offered that he and Michael would cook supper. "I mean Michael will cook and I will do what he tells me."

This gave Maggie an opportunity to talk with Father Gerald on her own. "Would you like to see the religion section at my store?" she asked.

"Sure," Father Gerald said, although it was clear that he knew it was just a ruse.

They walked over to the store followed by Olaf, and once they were inside, Maggie asked him if she could ask his advice about something confidential.

"Of course," he said and sat down in the upholstered chair near her desk.

Maggie moved her chair away from her desk so that there would be nothing between them, and she told Father Gerald about fleeing from her husband and not having seen or heard from him since. "The reason I'm telling you this" she explained a little belatedly "is that I know that Seamus is unhappy about our not being married. I hate his feeling that he's sinning by being with me. Is there any way that Seamus and I could marry without my having to locate Frank? It's been almost forty years. I hope he has died, but if he hasn't, I'd hate to let him know where I'm living. And what if he were to attack Seamus?" Maggie said no more for a moment trying to put out of her mind the image of Frank and Seamus fighting, Seamus thrown off balance because of his prosthesis.

Father Gerald interrupted those nightmare images. "Maggie, I've known Seamus a long time. "Your shared love is making him so happy that I wouldn't worry about the thorn on the rose of not being able to marry in the church."

"In the church?"

"According to the Roman Catholic Church if Frank is still alive you would need to have your first marriage annulled by Canon Law before you could marry again."

As Maggie nodded in discouragement, Father Gerald went on, "According to civil law, on the other hand, there is a legal form that you can post in the newspaper of whatever town you last saw him in, and if he doesn't respond within a certain amount of time you are considered legally divorced."

Maggie sighed as she settled back into her chair. "I've been afraid of Frank's finding me and the children for so long that the fear has gotten into my bones and stayed there even though he may be long dead, or, if alive, no longer interested in hurting me or finding the children."

"That's what lawyers are for," Father Gerald said gently. "Your lawyer posts the notice. Any response is sent to your lawyer. Your address is never revealed. And if by chance the response to your posting is that your husband has died, then you can be married in the Church."

At that moment Seamus opened the front door to the store

and announced with a flourish, "Spaghetti carbonara is served."

Chapter Sixty-two

Within a month, the lawyer Maggie hired, discovered that Frank had been dead for more than a decade. She'd been frightened of him all these years when he was solidly under the ground. She told Seamus the story, and announced that now that she was truly free, she very much wanted to marry him.

She wrote to Hannah in India who wrote back a congratulatory and loving letter, saying how glad she was that Michael was there to represent the family.

She wrote to Frankie in China who sent back a picture postcard of a high mountain that he was getting ready to climb. "Congratulations, I hope you're having as much fun as I'm having!"

Maggie told Seamus that she would like a small wedding, "Just the family. Do you think Gerald would be willing to preside despite my not being Catholic?"

"He told me he'd like nothing better."

Magdalena, who had become friends with Maggie while working in the upstairs office of the bookstore, offered her trailer as a place for the event. Magdalena's son, Carlos, was Seamus's godson so he and his parents were also family.

The afternoon of the day before the wedding Seamus and Maggie had their first fight. It was just past closing time. Maggie was using magic markers to make a sign to put in the window of the store the next day: *"Closed for the Day! Be Back Tomorrow"*

Seamus was getting ready to go back to his apartment in Hudson and make supper for Gerald who was driving down from Boston and spending the night with him. But as he was gathering his things, Seamus got a phone call on the bookstore phone. Although he was speaking in Spanish it seemed to Maggie that he was uncomfortable having her overhear his side of the conversation.

So when he hung up, she asked who he'd been talking to and what it was about.

It seemed to Maggie that Seamus winced at her question, but then he smiled as he seemed to summon up his courage to tell her. "That was Urbelino. He's hired a mariachi band for tomorrow."

"What!" The magic markers went flying as Maggie's hands went up into the air.

"Well, Maggie, listen, the point is... I mean what happened is... You see Urbelino told some friends about our wedding, and everyone kind of invited themselves to it. They brought over things to decorate the trailer with today They're bringing food and drink tomorrow. The weather is supposed to be perfect. Urbelino has a friend in a mariachi band and they turned out to be available.... and so they're coming."

Maggie stood up knocking over her chair. Ignoring the chair she said to the still seated Seamus, "But we decided on a small wedding! How can you change everything about our wedding, *our* wedding without asking me first?"

Seamus stood up and took both her hands in his. She tried to shake her hands free, but Seamus held on as he explained in the gentlest of voices, "This expansion of the wedding was not my idea nor even Urbelino's. Friends of Urbelino and Magdalena heard about it and assumed I'd, I mean we'd, be happy to have them celebrate with us. Except for the band, these are all people I know, people I've helped over the years. These are all good people. They want to meet you and celebrate with us. I think you'll enjoy..." He let go of her hands and put his arms round her waist. "I think you'll enjoy these people. I'm so proud of you and ...."

"But what about Joe and Sarah, and Joan, and Alejandro? How can you or Urbelino invite a bunch of people I don't even know and not invite the people I care about?"

"I'll call them this evening."

"But what will they think about such short..."

"I'll explain it all, how you wanted the wedding to be just the family and how it grew overnight. I better get going, Maggie; I don't want Gerald to arrive and not be there to let him in."

Maggie didn't want that to happen either. Father Gerald was making a long trip. But as Seamus stooped to gather his things she asked, "How on earth does one dance to a mariachi band?"

"I've no idea. We'll have to improvise. It will be our first challenge."

Maggie could think of nothing to say, so she gave him a kiss that left him panting, and closed the door on him.

But she was furious. She tried to concentrate on finishing the sign but misspelled "tomorrow". She tried to cover up her mistake, and made the whole thing look like a blob. *Maybe I'll just stay here and skip the wedding. It doesn't even sound like my wedding! Everyone will be speaking a language I don't understand!*

She stormed back to the house without locking the bookstore. At that moment the bookstore seemed to be her only friend, and she didn't want to lock it up.

At home she opened the bottle of wine she'd bought for their celebratory evening after the wedding, and poured herself a glass. And then she took the glass of wine, deciding after a moment to leave the bottle where it was, and went back to the store. She sat outside on the bench, leaned her back against the wall, and stared out across the road to the field on the other side. Olaf lay down at her feet. The sun was getting lower in the sky creating long shadows among the trees.

Finally she knew what to do. She went into the store to call. Malika answered, but as soon as she heard how upset Maggie sounded, she called to Caitlin to pick up on the second phone. Maggie told them how angry she was, and then she whined morosely, "I bought a beautiful pale green linen suit to be married in. I wanted to surprise you all with its beauty. The skirt is straight and just a bit too tight. I'll tear the seams if I try to dance in it."

"Come on over," Malika said. "We've got a closet full of costumes. We'll make you the most beautiful mariachi-dancing bride in the whole world."

"Do come," Caitlin said. "Aren't men impossible! Do you think Dad was planning to tell you before you got to the trailer? Come on over. We'll have fun."

Maggie began to cry as she got out the words, "I'm on my way."

Chapter Sixty-three

The morning was cloudy and smelled of rain coming at any moment. Seamus wondered what would happen if everyone had to fit into the trailer. He hadn't heard from Maggie since that last kiss. He told Gerald about the mariachi band, and asked if he thought Seamus should call Maggie to tell her again how sorry he was about the change of plans.

"I don't think so, Seamus. I think there's a reason that people say the groom shouldn't see the bride on the day of the wedding until the actual event. I would leave it."

"Not even a phone call?"

"Not even a phone call. Having presided over a great many weddings, I suggest you leave the bride and her entourage alone until she comes gloriously strolling down the aisle."

"I bow to your experience," Seamus told him, "and I hope to God you're right."

"Me too." Gerald said with a warm smile that made Seamus feel that they were brothers in arms.

Around 3:30 the clouds began to lift. When Gerald and Seamus arrived at the farm around 4:00, the sun was shining brilliantly on the many friends who were quickly setting up rows of chairs borrowed from every trailer in the area. The older children were blowing up balloons of many colors and tying one to each chair. The metal steps to the front of the trailer were already decorated with masses of yellow and white balloons.

By 4:45 every chair was occupied, and people stood, talking softly to each other beside and behind the rows of chairs. Children sat on the ground in front of the chairs, the older ones holding younger ones in their laps. Some children chased each other among the standing adults until they were picked up and held in people's arms.

At 5:00 Gerald took his place in front of the steps to the trailer facing the crowd. Seamus stood off to the side and asked Urbelino, who stood beside him, if he had the ring. It wasn't the first time Seamus had asked, and Urbelino simply smiled. Then Joe, who stood at the back, started to play a solo oboe version of Pachelbel's Canon.

Seamus turned around to see Maggie and Michael processing toward them down the center aisle between the chairs. On Maggie's head was a crown of flowers. Her dress was the color of the afternoon sky. She looked like the sunshine that had broken through the clouds and now enveloped them all. She had her hand in the crook of Michael's elbow. Michael wore a pale grey suit that Seamus had helped him buy for the occasion. He was smiling broadly. filled to the brim with sunny happiness.

When Maggie and Michael arrived at the front of the

trailer, Seamus turned to face Gerald who asked, "Who is presenting this woman to be married to this man?"

"I am," Michael said with authority, as if he were Maggie's father, instead of her grandson. He then kissed Maggie on the cheek, and turned to sit down in the front row.

The ceremony began! It felt to Seamus as though the air itself was alive and celebratory. As Gerald recited the prayers, his joyful face seemed to promise that the sun would continue to shine on them, no matter how dark the clouds became.

As Maggie and Seamus exchanged rings, they recited their intentions to remain together in sickness and in health, in wealth and in poverty, until the end of their days.

Then Gerald declared, smiling broadly, "I now pronounce you man and wife."

And their new life began with a kiss.

Joe began to play Bach's "Jesu, Joy of Man's Desiring." Seamus took Maggie's hand and they began to process up the aisle. Everyone was standing and smiling at them. Over the years Seamus had been advocating for these families in hospitals and schools, courts and job interviews. He loved having them with him on this day.

While he and Maggie were being hugged and congratulated, other guests quickly got to work to move the rows of chairs with their attached many-hued balloons into a wide circle. The mariachi band, in their splendid garb of black suits with bright red bowties and red cummerbunds, and broad-brimmed straw hats, stepped into the circle and began to play.

Children of all ages immediately began to hop and swirl to the music. Malika and Caitlin began a lively dance that made people stare with interest. For one second Seamus worried about what people might think, and then he let the worry go, he hoped for ever. He looked for Michael who was holding little James to his chest rocking back and forth with the music. Joan's granddaughter, Kari, began to do ballet twirls in the circle until she knocked over Urbelino's son, Carlos. She pulled him upright by both of his hands and the two of them created their own dance. Magdalena and Urbelino had stopped mid-dance to kiss. They looked almost like royalty having created this celebration.

Seamus saw one of the mariachi band members beckon to Joe to join them. Joe threw back his head as though laughing at the idea, but then, after a moment, he unearthed his oboe from its case and joined them, smiling shyly at first and then more and more happily as he found his way into their music.

When Joe left her side to join the mariachi band, Sarah looked around for someone she knew. She saw her mother and Alejandro dancing exuberantly. Sarah caught her breath and sat down on one of the chairs as she watched them. *Why was I hovering over her all the time? Look at her, she's fine! How could I have let those nurses tie her into the wheelchair? I was trying to keep her from falling. I was trying to keep her from embarrassing herself.* "Oh my God," she found herself whispering these words aloud, "I'm afraid of embarrassing my children by trying to dance when it's too late."

As she watched her mother and Alejandro kick up their heels, a girl, who was spinning around near them, fell. Joan and Alejandro stopped dancing, and Alejandro stooped and picked up the child to carry her out of the way of the dancers.

Sarah quickly pushed her way in among the dancers to where Joan was standing. She hugged Joan hard, and whispered into her ear, "I'm so sorry, Mom!"

Joan held her daughter closer still. "You were doing your best. I felt the same way about Grannie. It's not easy being the daughter of someone who's getting older."

At that moment Sam tapped Sarah on the shoulder, "Hey Mom, do you want to dance?"

"Yes, Sam, yes please."

As soon as Sarah and Sam danced off, Alejandro was back at Joan's side. The music had changed to something slow and Alejandro held her very close as they rejoined the dancers.

Seamus looked around for Maggie, but suddenly felt her hand in his.

"I like your friends," she told him.

"Keeping her hand in his, Seamus led her into the circle of dancers. Once inside, surrounded by friends and family, and inspired by the music that had celebrated festivities for centuries, Seamus put his arm around Maggie's waist, and held her close as he whispered into her ear, "Let's improvise."

Acknowledgments

This book was made possible by my family and friends surrounding me with help. My sister, Winslow, read many versions and gave good advice. My brother, Jefferson, designed and created the cover. My step-daughter, Rachel, and my cousin, Annie, were early helpful readers, as were my friends, Franny and Leslie. Leslie then became my final reader examining each word and phrase and helping me enormously by making the text ready to be shared. Rosemary Ahern was my editor for this book and *Surprised by Joy*. Her criticisms were astute and her enthusiastic support sustained me when I came close to giving up. I am filled with gratitude to you all!

www.ingramcontent.com/pod-product-compliance
Lightning Source LLC
Chambersburg PA
CBHW031311170626
46807CB00001B/378